MARCIE and the MONSTER OF THE BAYOU

Books by Betty Hager

The Gift of the Dove
Old Jake and the Pirate's Treasure
Miss Tilly and the Haunted Mansion
Marcie and the Shrimp Boat Adventure
Marcie and the Monster of the Bayou

Musicals by Betty Hager

Angels, Lambs, Ladybugs, and Fireflies
  (with Fred Bock)
A Super Gift from Heaven *(with Fred Bock)*
Three Wee Kings *(with Dan Sharp and
  Fred Bock)*
The Greatest Christmas Card in the Whole,
  Wide World *(with Fred Bock)*
O, My Stars, It's Christmas!
  (with Fred Bock and Anne Claire)
God with a Capital G *(with Fred Bock)*
The Mall and the Night Visitor
  (with Fred Bock)
God's Rainbow Promises of Christmas
  (with Fred Bock)
Hallelujah 1-4-8 *(with Fred Bock)*
Angels, Lambs, Caterpillars, and Butterflies
  (with Fred Bock)
Holiday Inn, Bethlehem *(with Fred Bock)*

MARCIE and the MONSTER OF THE BAYOU

BETTY HAGER

ZondervanPublishingHouse
Grand Rapids, Michigan

A Division of HarperCollinsPublishers

Marcie and the Monster of the Bayou
Copyright © 1994 by Betty Hager

Requests for information should be addressed to:
Zondervan Publishing House
Grand Rapids, Michigan 49530

Library of Congress Cataloging-in-Publication Data

Hager, Betty.
    Marcie and the monster of the bayou / Betty Hager.
        p.   cm. — (Tales from the bayou)
    Summary: An imaginative twelve-year-old has trouble when
she claims to have seen a sea monster in the bayou near her
house and when she tries to protect her new friend whose harelip
has made her the subject of malicious gossip.
    ISBN 0-310-38431-1 (paper)
    [1. Bayous — Fiction. 2. Cleft lip — Fiction. 3. Physically
handicapped — Fiction. 4. Friendship — Fiction. 5. Alabama
— Fiction.] I. Title. II. Series: Hager, Betty. Tales from the
bayou.
    PZ7.H12416Mar   1994   93–44490
    [Fic] — dc20   CIP
                                                  AC

Edited by Lori J. Walburg
Cover designed by Cindy Davis
Cover illustration by Doug Knutson
Interior illustrations by Craig Wilson, the Comark Group

Printed in the United States of America

94 95 96 97 98 99 / ❖DH/ 10 9 8 7 6 5 4 3 2 1

*For Patty, who has introduced
my books and musicals
to numerous children.*

Love and thanks

Contents

Contents

The Monster of the Bayou

I'm telling you the truth, Jeanné." I was insistent. "There is some kind of beast or dragon or *sea monster* in the bayou. I saw it with my own two eyes."

Jeanné smiled, frowned, and lifted her shoulders in disbelief. With an embarrassed giggle she said, "My goodness, Marcie. You see more with your two eyes than most folks see all their lives."

Jeanné was just about my best friend, and I could usually depend on her to believe me. That's why her sarcastic remark hurt.

People didn't think of me as being dishonest, but a lot of folks said my imagination was "amazingly colorful." Actually, those were my mama's words. When my papa thought I was giving an exaggerated account of some person or event, he'd say, "Marcie, honey, I'm afraid your imagination's a bit too hale and hearty."

I might have taken that to mean my imagination was healthy and, therefore, a good thing, but I suspected he meant the opposite. And now it looked like Jeanné agreed with him.

"Why, you oughta be ashamed," I said to her. "You know I don't make things up."

Jeanné's blue eyes wore an expression of constant sincerity, sort of like her personality. There was an appearance of regret in them now, mingled with a sort of "I give up."

"You know I always believe you, Marcie," she said, her voice as sincere as her eyes, "but it's just that, well, sometimes things have sort of . . . not been exactly like you thought they were."

I knew she meant "things" like the way I'd thought our Cajun friend, Mr. Jake, was a ghost. That's before I got to know him, of course. And she remembered how I had been "dead sure" the old lady who lived in the haunted-looking house across the bayou was a witch. Instead, Miss Tilly became a good friend of mine. And Jeanné's.

"You aren't being fair," I said, sincere, too; I was defending my reputation. "There were situations and events that caused me to believe those things. Besides, you, and Raymie, and Hank, and Pierre, well, y'all believed just as much as I did."

Something in her eyes made me add, "Well, almost as much."

There was nothing easy about convincing Jeanné or anyone else that right here in our own bayou, I had seen a monster.

Our house was just across the white, crushed oyster-shell road from the bayou. Papa's Marine Hardware and Supply Store was on the bayou. Its tar-blackened wharf jutted out above its waters.

About a hundred yards from the shop, a huge and very old oak tree bent over the bayou. I liked to sit under that tree when I was bored or lonely.

Well, I didn't sit there *only* when I was bored and lonely. Sometimes I liked sitting in that spot because I enjoyed being there. The old, exposed roots provided a comfortable place to sit. There was a beautiful view of the bayou from the oak, and sometimes interesting events took place there. I had once watched a fishing boat catch fire and burn itself right down into the water. As terrible as that was for the owner, seeing the leaping orange flames above the dark water had been beautiful and exciting.

I'd watch the boats go by, too. There were the boats that came to "oil up" before going out into Portersville Bay or the Gulf of Mexico to shrimp or fish. Sometimes pleasure boats would pass by. They were sleek, white, and graceful. On board were men from Mobile or other cities. They came to our little fishing town of Bayou La Batre, Alabama, to rent boats for pleasure fishing.

My sixteen-year-old brother, Raymie, didn't have to go to school in the summer. I liked to watch my father and him as they worked. They'd come out on the wharf to pump gas and oil for the boats. They'd laugh and joke with the fishermen.

Raymie was sunbrowned; the girls at the high school said he was handsome. When he wasn't teasing me, I thought he was handsome, too. True, that didn't leave much time for admiring him.

I don't suppose a person could say Papa was handsome but, to me, he was the best-looking man in the world. He was tall, and ruddy, and white-haired, and his blue eyes continually sparkled. Almost continually. When he was angry they'd turn a steel grey. They were blue most of the time; it took a lot to make Papa angry.

Sometimes, when returning from a trip, one of the men would come off his boat with oysters, or shrimp, or fish. He'd give Papa a bucket or two and say, "Hey, Isaac! Maybe Miss Helene would like to make a little gumbo for supper."

And, sometimes, if there were oysters, Papa would call over to me at my perch on the oak roots.

"Hey, Marcie. Go up to the house and get an oyster knife and some ketchup and hot sauce. And bring some crackers, too, would you, please?"

The men would sit on the wharf and enjoy jokes with their oysters and crackers. I liked getting things ready for Papa's little "oyster feast," but my stomach would be queasy when I saw

Papa and the men swallowing those oysters, whole and raw. I never did develop a taste for raw oysters.

That's how I came to see the *monster of the bayou* that summer of 1934. I was sitting under my oak, playing with the fiddler crabs. The day was hot and humid, a typical summer day in August. I wore shorts and a halter top, but I still couldn't keep cool in the constant Alabama sun. The rays burned into my skin, and the sheltering leaves of the oak brought little relief.

I was wishing I could go for a swim over at Willow Creek, but I could go only if Raymie went with me. Mama figured, just because Raymie was sixteen, he could save me from drowning. But Raymie couldn't go. Papa needed him in the shop that day.

I leaned against the tree and was almost asleep, my eyes half closed as I imagined how the scene across the bayou would look if an artist painted and framed it. I admired the dark green marsh grass. Scattered in the marsh were small coffee bean trees heavy with wisteria-shaped orange blossoms. There was a clearing of crushed oyster shells on the shoreline where fishermen sometimes tarred and repaired their nets. A scattering of small, greyed shacks were sprinkled among several scrub pines, and further away, in the yards of small white houses, deep pink crepe myrtle trees and glossy, green pines stood sharply against the blue sky.

My daydreaming was shattered when I heard Mr. Luis Delacruz's boat, *The Lillie Mae,* passing by. That little shrimp lugger was hitting all cylinders as its bow cleaved the waters. The sharp division of the water made a white, foamy spray. When a boat with enough power moved at a fast clip, it would cut a wide and forceful wake.

I sat up, hoping to see my fourteen-year-old friend, Pierre, on board. Sometimes he went out fishing with his dad and older brother. If he were on the boat he must have been in the cabin. Mr. Delacruz was at the wheel of the pilot house and Thomas was at the mast, busy doing something with the ropes.

Just then I saw something that made me forget all about Pierre. It was a monster— writhing and leaping in the boat's wake.

I leaped to my feet, a hand to my heart, the other placed on my face in dismay. I was too shocked at first to make a sound other than a soft, wavering, "Ohhhh."

When I realized I had seen a sea monster, I pointed and screamed to Papa and the men on the wharf, "Papa! Everybody, look! A dragon!"

I must have caught their attention, because all four of the men stood and looked. But *The Lillie Mae* had passed and left only the waters lapping against the shores on both sides. There was no strange creature in sight.

"What'd you see?" Papa called over to me.

My heart was beating at a fast clip. My hands were cold. I could scarcely speak as I called to him, "A monster. There was a *sea monster*, Papa."

Papa looked at me for a long moment, sighed, and sat back down. The other men looked after *The Lillie Mae*, now far up the bayou. Seeing nothing, they turned to Papa for a quizzical moment. Then they dropped to their places on the wharf again.

Papa looked over at me, shaking his head. "Y'all will have to excuse my daughter," he said. "I'm afraid her imagination is a bit too hale and hearty at times."

He was smiling, but I couldn't mistake a certain sound of disgust, tinged with disbelief, in his voice.

"Yeah," Mr. John Walsh said. "My Margaret's in the same grade with Marcie."

From my distance I strained to hear. His words weren't completely clear, but I heard enough.

I think he said, "Margaret says your girl can write a story as good as any of them famous New York writers."

"Yeah, she'll probably put those tall tales on paper some day and get 'em published," Papa said.

I was too embarrassed to enjoy compliments, and I was hurt. How could Papa do this to me? I got up, straightened my shoulders, and huffed off, my head in the air, my lips pressed together tightly in disappointment.

Midway across the road I turned to look at them. They had gone back to their oyster opening and eating. They had forgotten me. I was offended.

In honesty, I have to say I understood their doubt. No one had ever seen a sea monster. That is, no one I had ever known.

I had lived on this bayou all my life and had never had so much as a glimpse of such a creature. But then, what had I just seen?

It has to be a monster, I thought. *Why, it must have been at least . . . twelve or fifteen feet long. And . . . and it wiggled and waved, just like the sea monsters and dragons in book illustrations.*

That was when I'd gone to the wall telephone on our back porch and furiously turned the handle to call Jeanné. She came over right away, but her visit disappointed me. Like I said, this was the first time I had ever known her to doubt me.

I wanted to show her what I had seen. I figured when there were several boats going down the bayou there'd be a chance to see a big wake again. I reasoned that whatever that creature was, the boat disturbing the water must anger him.

Jeanné and I watched until supper time and she had to go home. The monster hadn't shown up again that day. Jeanné looked at me with disappointment and doubt.

"Well, see you," she said.

The slight wave of her fingers, and the turned-down corners of her mouth declared her disappointment in me.

While we were eating supper that evening Papa told Mama and Raymie about my "pulling some stunt about a bayou monster." He wasn't angry or making fun. I believe he thought the incident was funny, now he'd had time to think about it. Nothing about it was funny to me.

Of course, Raymie teased me.

"Boy, oh, boy, Marcie!" he hooted. "This tops 'em all. A sea monster, huh? Whoo-ee!"

I was incensed.

"I know what I saw!" I cried out, furious. "And it just so happens I remember when you didn't believe we had a stowaway on the boat with us last spring, Smarty Pants."

Surely he remembered how *I* had been the one to discover the little four-year-old stowaway, Ulysses, when we'd gone out shrimping on *Miss Pretty Pelican.*

Mama put a warning hand on my arm as she said, "Not so loud, honey. There's no reason to yell, you know."

She picked up a few dishes and pushed away from the table with a gesture of finality, sweetly adding, "You know, I do think you saw something. But, you have to admit, it's very difficult for us to believe you saw a . . . a *sea monster.*"

I lowered my voice and said, "I'm gonna prove this to y'all if it's the last thing I ever do."

My shoulders were up, my chin was up, and my sense of unfairness was definitely up.

Convincing
the Doubters

Proving I had seen a bayou monster wasn't as easy as I had hoped. I spent most of my August afternoons that summer at the oak or sitting on Papa's wharf. I'd take a tall thermos of iced tea down with me and a Coca Cola fan, the kind with the wooden stick on the end and a painting of young men and women having fun. Those August days were almost unbearably hot. Mama said three teaspoons of sugar in my thermos wouldn't help me stay cool.

"Sugar's like a fuel. You're just warming yourself up. Why don't you take water, honey?"

Mama was trying to be nice to me about the ogre, as she called the bayou monster. I knew she was humoring me, and that only made me more determined. I didn't know how I was going to do this, but I was going to see that someone, anyone, would get a glimpse of that monster.

Raymie and his friend, Hank, called the monster my "bogeyman."

Hank, pushing his red hair back from his forehead, his entire freckled face grinning, would say, "Hey, Marcie, seen your bayou bogeyman lately?"

Raymie would guffaw and hold his sides with laughter.

I decided I wouldn't cater to their teasing. I lifted my shoulders and walked away, head in air.

Sometimes I'd take my latest library books down to the oak. I wouldn't be able to concentrate, though. Every time a boat would pass, even a speedboat, I'd look up and carefully watch the wake. I was determined to prove my truthfulness.

One day Mr. Luis Delacruz came to buy a monkey wrench and a pair of pliers from Papa. His son, Pierre, was with him. I was obsessed with proving the monster, and I was glad to see him.

Mama said Pierre's tales were almost as wild and foolish as mine. I guess that's one reason why I liked Pierre. That, his big, brown eyes, and the way his dark hair curled about his face. Jeanné said he was my boyfriend. That made me mad. He was a *boy*, and he was a *friend*, but he wasn't my *boyfriend*.

"Good gracious, Jeanné," I'd say. "I'm only twelve."

Papa and Mr. Luis got to talking so Pierre and I had a long visit. Pierre and I spotted each other when he and his dad first drove up. I was sitting at my usual place under the oak. He came over to talk with me.

"Whatcha doin', Shrimp?" he asked.

That annoyed me. I knew he'd called me that because he'd heard Raymie and Hank. I didn't like hearing that from him. He was almost three years older than I, and I was proud that he treated me like a friend.

"Whatcha doing, *Catfish*?" I asked, my tone sarcastic.

He must have been sorry, because he quickly said, "How's everything going with you?"

I had heard a shrimp barrel worth of lessons about forgiveness in Sunday school, so I forgave him. Besides, I wanted to talk about the monster. Naturally, I told Pierre everything. I began to remember things about that monster I hadn't realized.

"Lemme tell you something, Pierre," I said, warming to my tale, "he had a red tongue, or if it wasn't a tongue, I'm pretty sure there was a flame."

"Couldn't be a flame," he said. "Remember, he was in water."

I felt superior. I had read a lot more fiction than Pierre, even though I was younger.

"It's different with monsters and dragons," I informed him. "Their fire doesn't go out just because of a little ole water."

He shrugged. "Maybe," he conceded. "Okay, how long would you say the, uh, dragon, or whatever, was?"

He didn't want to admit he was getting excited, but I could tell. That inspired me.

"About twenty or twenty-five feet," I said. "Maybe twenty-eight."

"Goodness," he breathed. I could see he was getting interested. "What'd she look like?"

"He was really ugly," I said. I wasn't going to call that fearful monster a female.

"How big 'round would you guess?"

I held my hands in a circle, as wide as I could, as I said, "Oh, maybe a couple of feet in diameter."

"Did she have a tail, or a horny spine, or anything like that?"

I thought a moment, trying to remember. After all, seeing that creature had jolted me. People couldn't remember every detail when they'd been in shock. I had been in shock that time I'd sprained my ankle and could scarcely remember how the accident had happened.

"I think he had a sort of scraggly tail," I mused.

"Pointed spines?"

"Nah." I thought about it. "More like humps, I think."

"Camel humps?"

I could see he was teasing again. "No, silly!" I said. "Smooth humps, but not pointed spines."

"What color was she?"

I was becoming annoyed. "You know, Pierre, I haven't said one word about that monster being a *girl*!"

He grinned.

"Well," I said, teasing back, "I'm not sure what color *he* was, but I'm sure there was a monster."

He shook his head. "I don't know, Marcie. I don't think there could be a monster in the bayou. Maybe in one of those big lakes somewhere, but not in a bayou . . ."

I was alarmed. What was happening to Pierre, my "imagination partner"?

Papa and Mr. Luis were standing at the door of the shop. I hadn't been able to convince my one possible ally. I hoped they'd talk longer. I had the distinct feeling Pierre Delacruz was growing up and beginning to leave his imagination somewhere in the eighth grade.

But I was in luck. At just that moment, a miracle happened. Mr. Billy Jim Boisonot's big, fifty-foot shrimp lugger came chugging by at high speed. Pierre remembered when I had gone out on that boat as part of the shrimp crew with Mr. Jake, Hank, and Raymie that past spring. We both turned to look.

I was excited. *Miss Pretty Pelican* had a lot of power. I was sure there'd be a vigorous wake.

I wasn't disappointed.

When the sea monster rose from the bayou depths I screamed and leaped up. "Look!" I pointed.

"I—I can't believe it," Pierre gasped. He whirled around to face Papa and Mr. Luis and called out in a voice packed with amazement, "Did y'all see that?"

I sighed with joy. Sometimes life has a knack for fulfilling a person's wishes in a very satisfying way.

The Leviathan

I was certain Papa would believe me if I could produce even one witness. I grabbed Pierre's hand, and we both rushed across the grassy mound separating the tree and the shop.

"You see, Papa," I cried, stumbling over my words as well as my feet as we ran to the door of the shop. "Did you hear Pierre? I wasn't making it up. There really, truly *is* a bayou monster."

Papa wasn't at all impressed. His blue eyes glimmered with a held-back smile as he gave one of those adult conspiracy looks to Pierre's father.

"Luis, get an earful of this," he said.

Mr. Luis didn't have even an inkling of what we were saying. He was a dark, skinny little man, almost bald, with a fringe of brownish-grey hair about his head and a bony face, shaped like President Lincoln's. When he was a boy, he must have looked a lot like Pierre. His eyes were still big and brown, but the skin was wrinkled now.

He was a Cajun from Louisiana, like our friend, Mr. Jake, who lived in the shed in back of our house.

"*Monstre de mer*?" he asked, puzzled. That meant sea monster in French.

"Honest!" I said, drawing a cross on my heart with my pointer finger. "Really and truly, Mr. Luis."

The two men turned to look at one another. Both of them burst out laughing.

Papa shook his head and looked at Pierre. "Son," he said, "I can't believe you let her talk you into this."

Pierre wouldn't look at me. "Well, there was something. But a sea monster? I don't know."

"Why, Pierre Delacruz!" I shrieked. "You know you saw that—that—thing as well as I did!"

Pierre drew circles in the dirt with his toes. He didn't look at me once.

"I heard you yelling to Papa and your father," I said, irate now. "There was definitely a sea monster in that bayou, and you saw it."

"Yeah, sure," my papa said. "Dead marsh water, flotsam and jetsam, old tin cans, a few inedible catfish—"

"—Papa," I protested, "you're making fun of me."

My papa wasn't one to make fun of children, or anyone else for that matter. He put his hands on my shoulders and soberly said, "I'm sorry."

He turned to Pierre. "What did you see, son?"

Mr. Luis, following Papa's example, choked back a chuckle and tried to keep his expression straight.

Pierre was confused. He gestured toward the bayou.

"Well—I—there was—well—*something* in the bayou there . . ."

The two men, trying hard to listen with respect, looked at him with questions in their eyes.

Papa said, "Yes?" at the same time Mr. Luis said, "*Oui?*"

Pierre finished lamely, "Well . . . I guess it *looked* like a sea monster, but it must have been our imagination."

I was disgusted with him for letting the men make him back down in this way. I placed my fists on my hips and said, "It *was* a sea monster, and it *wasn't* my imagination."

My eyes filled with unexpected tears, embarrassing me. Of all people, I didn't want Pierre to see me cry. Too late.

I wheeled about and started running across the road to our house.

My voice held the beginning of a strangled sob as I called back, "I better go help Mama with supper."

Pierre called, "Bye, Marcie."

I waved without turning around, my eyes blinded with tears. I wondered if Pierre would deny what he'd seen to everyone.

The monster was the main topic of conversation at supper that night again. Papa wasn't making fun of me, but I knew he was far from convinced. Raymie was downright rude until Mama told him, "Hold your tongue."

"Marcie, whatever you saw," she said, "I'm certain you thought it looked like a monster, but really, honey, remember how you were just positive Miss Tilly was a witch, even when Papa and I told you how silly such thinking was?"

I was seething with frustration. We had fried shad roe and browned potatoes for supper, two of my favorite dishes, but I had lost my appetite.

"Mama," I said, my mouth full of the golden fish eggs, "I don't mean to talk back to you, but you're wrong. This is different. You gotta believe me."

Raymie said, "Close your mouth when you eat, stupid. You're making me sick to my stomach. I think I'm gonna throw up."

"Close your own mouth!" I flared at him. I turned back to Mama, my feelings injured.

She placed a quieting hand firmly on both of our arms. She was definitely annoyed with us.

"I'm sorry," I said, not sure I meant it, "but, Mama, this—this—thing is about thirty-five feet long, and it has a long tail, and a—a red flame of fire coming out of its mouth."

I hated the way she'd sometimes twist her mouth to keep from smiling about me. I felt even worse when I saw her sneak a hand under the table and squeeze Papa's knee.

I was ready to object. I was going to say, "I saw that, Mama," but Raymie started teasing in earnest.

He pursed his lips as if he were talking to a tiny baby and shook his head back and forth as he cooed, "Oh, de poor wittle babykins. De big, bad dwagon gonna cwoss de road and come get our wittle sweetie pie tonight. Don't worry, lambkins, your big, brave brudder, Waymie, he gonna take care of you."

"Papa," I wailed, "make him stop."

"That's right, Raymie," Papa commanded. "That'll be enough!"

When Papa sounded that way, we obeyed. For the time being, Raymie stopped his teasing, but when we were alone I knew he'd tease again.

Actually, Raymie was a nice big brother. Most of the time, I loved him. Mama said I teased him just as much as he teased me. I suppose I did. I know I could get him furious when I teased him about "showing off" for the girls when we went swimming at Willow Creek.

But I was really aggravated with him over that monster. I knew I'd seen something, and I was certain the creature I'd seen wasn't some invention I'd called up in my head. I couldn't wait to see Pierre again to make him tell me what *he'd* seen. Turns out, I got my chance sooner than I'd thought.

One Sunday afternoon, Jeanné and Hank came over for dinner. Jeanné had gone to early

29

mass at St. Bridget's Catholic Church, and Hank and our family had gone to Sunday school and church at the First Baptist Church.

We were sitting at the dining room table. The room was small, but when the table was open there was room for ten people. The table almost covered the entire area.

There were seven of us that Sunday, counting Mr. Jake. He usually ate with us when he got home from St. Bridget's. Papa had just finished saying the blessing, and we were anxious to start eating. As each bowl was passed my mouth watered in expectation.

We had homemade biscuits, fig preserves, mashed potatoes, freshly snapped green beans, corn on the cob, and golden brown, crisply fried chicken. I had snapped the beans myself, just before we went to Sunday school.

There was a knock at the door.

Papa said, "Answer that, will you, Marcie?"

I slipped over to open the door, just a few feet away from where I sat.

Pierre Delacruz stood at the door. He had on his blue seersucker Sunday pants, a starched white shirt, and a striped tie.

He was twisting a white cap nervously in his hands.

He looked at everyone around the table. I could tell he was shy and embarrassed about interrupting our Sunday dinner.

As soon as Mama heard Pierre's voice she stood up, walked around the table to the door, and took Pierre's arm. Mama especially liked Pierre. She had a warm place in her heart for him because his mama had died and he lived with his papa and older brother.

"Why, if it isn't our young friend, Pierre," she said. "Come on in and eat dinner with us, honey."

"Oh, no, ma'am, I couldn't," Pierre protested.

I knew he wished he could disappear under the floorboards of the front porch. I'd have felt the same way in his place. I was torn between feeling sorry for him and being irritated as I thought of how he'd let me down about the monster of the bayou.

"Nonsense," Mama said. "Isaac, make a place for Pierre over by you there. Raymie, get another plate and some utensils."

Everyone shifted and moved, or whatever it took to include Pierre. Mama had put a couple of electric fans on the floor to cool us off. There were two big pitchers of iced tea on the buffet, and everyone was feeling contented and sociable. Before we knew it, Pierre was having a good time.

Jeanné punched my ribs and whispered, "See. He *is* your boyfriend."

That disturbed me. I rewarded her with a quick jab back.

"He is not!" I hissed. Luckily, everyone was so noisy no one heard us.

Papa said we could make ice cream after dinner. He had the freezer ready with chipped ice and rock salt, and he'd already covered it with burlap sacks to keep the ice from melting.

I couldn't help teasing Raymie a little.

"Too bad your girl isn't here to sit on the freezer while you turn the handle, Raymie."

He must have been in a good mood, because he said, "Yeah, Marcie. You're so skinny we might as well have a feather sit on the freezer for all the good you'll do. We'll probably need both you and Jeanné to be heavy enough for us to turn the handle."

That's when Pierre made the remark that made me want to kiss him. Well, not really *kiss*. But I was able to do a lot of forgiving in the blink of an eye.

First, he looked at Mama and said, "That was a mighty fine Sunday dinner, Miss Helene. Thank you for asking me."

And then he looked around the table at everyone. He looked at Papa first, but his eyes stopped on Raymie and Hank as he said, "The reason I came over here was to tell y'all that Marcie is right. There really *is* a monster in the bayou, and it ain't just her imagination."

He turned to look at me, a frank and honest gaze of apology, but when I looked back at him in thankfulness he got timid and shyly dropped his gaze.

His words were soft but distinct when he said, "I'm sorry about the other day. I—I guess, now I'm getting older, I'm getting tired of folks telling me I'm making things up. Well, when Mr. Isaac and my papa looked like they were laughing at us, I—I just couldn't admit I'd seen it . . . the—the—monster."

Papa was more surprised than anyone. He put his fork down, pushed his chair away from the table, folded his arms, and leaned back. I think Pierre's earnest manner convinced him to show respect.

"I'm the one to be sorry," Papa said. "You see, that's a mighty wild story for modern men like your papa and me to believe, but I can see that you think you saw something. Maybe you oughta tell us a little more, son."

My honor was restored. I was cleared of my crime. I jumped up from my seat and threw my arms in the air. I whirled in circles around the table, all the while crying out in victory to everyone who'd listen, "I tole you so! I tole you so! See? Pierre saw it, too. Did you hear?"

Papa told me to sit down.

Now that someone else had agreed with me, I was filled with enthusiasm. We finished our fine Sunday dinner. Mama suggested we go outside and freeze the ice cream while we discussed our monster.

"There must have been some reason why both of you are so positive," she said.

I can't say Pierre and I completely convinced everyone, but I knew we had them interested. They were full of questions. What color? How big around? How long?

"About forty feet," I said.

"Oh, come on," Raymie chided. "It couldn't be that big. How big do you think it was, Pierre?"

Pierre was careful with my feelings now. I know he felt bad about not standing up with me in front of his father and Papa.

He sort of stuttered, "Why—why—I can't say, Raymie. We got such a quick look we can't be sure . . ."

"I don't know," Raymie pondered. "'Course I don't believe in monsters, but I can understand you did see something. I'm wondering if an unusually big shark didn't come in from the Gulf?"

"I don't know, either," Pierre said, "but it didn't seem like a shark at all. It was too long."

Jeanné said, "Even if there is such a thing as a sea monster, I *know* science can prove that fire won't burn when something's wet. I'm positive of that. I'm not saying you're fibbing, Marcie and Pierre, but you do know that's a fact."

I knew she was right, but I didn't know how to answer her doubts. I remembered the red flame vividly.

"Maybe the red something was a tongue," Hank suggested.

Pierre gave me a quick glance before he said, "Yeah, maybe he's right. Maybe he had a tongue."

Papa looked at Mama. In a deep, low voice he gave a not-quite-exact quote from the King James version of the Bible: "The Lord with his great and strong sword shall punish leviathan, the piercing serpent, that crooked serpent; and he shall slay the dragon that is in the sea."

I thought I saw him give Mama a wink when he'd finished the quote. His eye closed so briefly and so quickly I wasn't sure, but when Mama intoned, "Yea, verily," I knew for a fact he'd given her that crafty wink.

That little fun between Mama and Papa really got to me. I sincerely hoped I'd get the chance to prove to them there really was a dragon, or serpent, or ogre, or bogeyman, or sea monster, or, yes, a *leviathan* in our bayou.

A Town on Fire
with Rumors

More than anyone else, I wanted Raymie and Hank to see the monster. Maybe Mama and Papa would believe us if these older boys could tell them they'd seen it.

I continued to keep my watch by the bayou. Raymie would wave at me from the wharf. He'd grin and yell and call out, "Had any sightings yet?"

He was only half serious, so that's why I was thrilled when my chance finally came a few days later. The pleasure boat *Lovely Lady* was coming up from the mouth of the bayou. That meant they had already gathered their momentum, so they were approaching at full speed. Luckily, Raymie was on the wharf. Here was a possible opportunity.

"Hey!" I called out. "Raymie!"

I pointed at the *Lovely Lady*. I didn't have to tell him what I meant. He laughed but he swivelled about to watch.

That sleek *Lady* sliced through the bayou at a fast rate, and the waters spread out behind, exactly as I had hoped.

There it was! The monster of the bayou! And in the same way it had happened before, the creature slipped under the water as soon as the boat was gone.

I was thrilled. I was overjoyed. I jumped about, clapping my hands, gasping with delight.

"Did you see him? Did you see him?" I screamed over and over and over.

Raymie just stood there, looking after the boat, a stunned expression on his face. He spoke so softly I couldn't hear from that distance, so I shrieked, "Well, answer me, Dunderhead!"

He walked down the slanted boards of the wharf toward me, shaking his head in disbelief. I met him halfway, crazy with excitement.

"Well?" I said. I wanted him to say something. I wanted to hear him admit I'd been right.

He said, "I didn't see anything, shrimp."

I was furious with disappointment. I pounded on his chest with my fists.

"You did, too! You did, too!" I cried.

He caught my hands and laughed.

"Marcie. I'm just teasing."

"Why, that's the meanest ..." I started to say.

But he quickly continued, "You're right, Marcie." He shook his head in wonder. "There's something down there. I don't know what it is, but I saw something, and yeah, it does look like a sea monster. But, aw, I can't believe it was a monster, Marcie."

"Let's go tell Papa," I said. "Right now!"

He grinned, and the two of us went to the door of the shop. I felt as if popcorn were going off in my insides. I couldn't hold my excitement in. For a while there I didn't give Raymie a chance to get a word in edgewise.

Papa was behind the counter, straightening the shop, and Tom Henson was going through a bin of nails, choosing sizes.

"Papa!" I shouted. "The *Lovely Lady* just went by, going really fast, and Raymie saw it, and there was the sea monster, and, and . . . You tell him, Raymie."

Papa was smiling, puzzled. I wasn't making sense, I suppose. I stopped talking, feeling foolish.

Tom Henson was staring at me with an expression of curious amazement on his face. He was a wiry little man, about twenty-five years old. His hair was a shock of yellow straw, almost green from years of salt water and sun. His eyes were yellow-green, too, and his skin darkly sun-browned and rough looking.

Papa looked at Tom and back at me with a quick, meaningful glance. He seemed to be making some sort of gesture at me behind Tom's

back. Later I realized he'd wanted us to wait until Tom was gone before we told our story, but neither Raymie nor I got the message.

Raymie said, "Papa, I know this is crazy, and I know you're gonna think I'm as full of wild tales as Marcie and Pierre, but there really is—I mean, well, I think there is—a—a sea monster in the bayou."

He was embarrassed to be believing this wild story. He finished lamely, "'Course I know it can't be true, but . . ."

Papa said, "Oh, now come on, Raymie. Not you, too?"

Tom Henson was crazy with excitement. He grabbed Raymie's arm and said, "Where'd you see it? You mean a real monster? I always knowed there was something bad in the bayou. How big was it? What color was it, huh?"

I was thrilled to have someone believe me with such interest and emotion, but Raymie backed away as if he were concerned.

I felt it was my duty to tell this story. "I saw him right out by the wharf here," I said, "and I've seen him twice before this. He's really big, maybe fifty feet, and he has a red flame coming out of his mouth, and a straggly tail . . ."

Tom looked at Raymie and asked, "You seen it?"

That offended me, but I was anxious to have an ally, so I shook my head vigorously and said, "Tell him, Raymie."

By now Raymie must have caught on to why Papa didn't want us to say too much in front of Tom.

He said, "Well, it—it, well, it looked like a sea monster, but you have to realize, Tom, we never have seen a real live sea monster. So, uh, you know, we don't have anything to base it on."

Tom was so excited he could scarcely control himself. His eyes fluttered and his mouth twitched.

He shrieked, "Is that so? A real sea monster, huh? Sounds like we is all gonna be in bad trouble here in the bayou. I've heard them sea monsters cast a spell on folks—"

Papa interrupted, "—Nah, Tom, I don't think we have anything to worry about. The kids aren't sure of what they've seen."

Tom Henson ignored him. He was agitated, and his hands nervously plucked at his clothes.

"Listen, Mr. Isaac, I'll be back later for them nails. I ain't found the ones I want yet."

He looked at Raymie and me.

"A sea monster, huh? I'm gonna have to see that there monster for myself."

He rushed out the door, slamming it behind him.

Papa said, "Honestly, you two are a real pair. You know what's liable to happen now, don't you?"

"No," I said.

Raymie said, "What?

"That poor ignorant fella's the biggest trouble-maker in all of Bayou La Batre. His very name is Trouble. And Rumor Spreader. And Hate Monger. Did you see how his eyes lit up? Twenty minutes ago he told me he needed those nails right now, and here y'all came in with that story, and he's on fire to get out of here and tell the world."

Raymie and I looked at one another in surprise. Our papa wasn't a man to say untruthful or unkind things about anyone. When he talked like this, there had to be a reason.

Papa sighed. "Hey, I didn't mean to get on you two. What do you really think it was, Raymie?"

"It was a sea monster," I threw in, "like I tole you, and—"

"—Marcie," Papa interrupted. "I asked Raymie." He smiled at me as he added, "I've heard your story."

After Raymie had told all he knew, with me throwing in a helpful remark along the way, we had Papa seriously thinking something was in that bayou.

"But a *sea monster*?" he pondered. "That's hard to believe."

Thanks to Raymie and me not knowing when to keep our mouths shut, and thanks to Troublemaker Tom, things started hopping around Papa's Marine Hardware and Supply Shop. In some ways, it was good for business. Many people came to perch on "my" oak tree to get a sight of the sea monster. Some of the more pushy folks actually ran up on Papa's wharf when a boat was going by, for a better view.

Things really got bad when Tom Henson himself, along with a few friends, actually saw the monster.

At first, I was happy they'd seen my dragon. I was pleased with all the excitement. I told the story of my three sightings with great drama, throwing in all the suspense I could muster, enjoying the enthusiastic audiences.

But after awhile, affairs sort of got out of hand. One of the local restaurants set up a stand with boiled shrimp and hot sauce for sale. Mama was so upset over the mess some people were making across the street from her house she set out a wastebasket to take care of the trash. People were selling soft drinks and peanuts. The peanut shells made a mess, too.

Mama wouldn't let me go down to the bayou or the wharf. I thought she was being terribly unfair. I sat on our front porch to watch and listen.

Mama's cousin, we called her Cuddin Cassie, told Mama that Tom Henson was telling anyone who'd listen that some evil person was causing this monster to show up in the bayou, and he was going to find out who it was.

Cuddin Cassie said Tom told a group of men down at Mr. Tolly Breame's Ice Plant, "Y'all take my word for it. Them monsters don't come into no bayou unless they is some evil person casting a spell. They ain't no telling what kinda bad things Bayou La Batre is in store for."

Well, we took Tom Henson's ravings with a grain of salt, but later we had reason to remember the gossip and dangerous untruths he had started.

Frankie Fedora

As satisfying as it was to know I hadn't imagined the bayou monster, I was beginning to tire of all the excitement. I would have given anything to have seen that dragon caught and strung out on shore so we could prove, once and for all, there really was a sea monster in our own bayou.

I wanted it to end; people were getting rowdy and disorderly. So when Mama told me a new eleven-year-old girl had moved to town and she wanted me to meet her, I was pleased to have something new to think about. The girl's name was Frankie Fedora.

"That's a silly name," I said. "Frank's a boy's name, and doesn't *fedora* mean *hat*?"

"Right on both questions," she said. "She's called 'Frankie' because she's named after her mother, Frances. Now, run and wash up. Lunch is just about ready."

After lunch, Raymie drove us out to the Fedora farm on the highway. Mama said Mrs. Fedora would drive us back home. Mama had never learned to drive.

On the way, Mama told us about Frankie. Her family had moved here from New Orleans to grow tung oil trees. The nuts from the trees had small kernels inside that held oil, which was used in varnishes, paints, and lacquers.

"Did the Fedoras buy the land?" I asked. I figured if they had, they must be very rich. Nobody I knew had much money during the Depression.

"No," Mama said. "They're leasing it. They want to do what's best for their daughter. It's very difficult for Frankie to make new friends."

"What's wrong with her?" I asked. Making friends was easy for me.

Mama paused a moment before she said, "Frankie has a harelip."

"What in tarnation is a harelip?" I asked.

She explained the word comes from the fact that a person who is born with a harelip actually has a split lip, and the lip looks like a bunny's, or hare's, mouth.

Raymie snickered, and the thought of a person having a mouth that looked like a bunny's made me giggle, too; I couldn't help it.

Mama didn't scold us. She let us get our laugh over before she said, "That's why I wanted to be sure I talked to you about this before you saw her. I want to be certain you don't laugh or maybe stare at her."

She told us that only one side of Frankie's lip was split, that some people have two splits.

"It makes their mouths look strange, maybe even a little funny, but it isn't funny to people who are born that way. It also affects the way they speak, because the lip is shorter at the place where it's split. Frankie has a terrible time meeting people. Her mother and I decided it would be nice if she met several of you girls before school started next month."

Mama was volunteering at the library the morning she'd met Mrs. Fedora. Mrs. Fedora had come in to get some books for Frankie, and she told Mama all about her daughter.

"Mama," I said, "I'm afraid I'll laugh. I mean, I wouldn't wanna laugh, but sometimes—"

"—I know," Mama said. "Being nervous about things like this makes us laugh sometimes, but I believe you'll be all right. Just remember how bad it would make Frankie feel."

Raymie dropped us off at the Fedoras; he had to get back to work. We paused for a moment before we started up the zinnia-lined brick walk. I'd seen this house often when we were driving on the highway toward Mobile; it was a much bigger and finer house than ours. The entire house was made of used brick and trimmed in white wood. I thought it was beautiful.

Mrs. Fedora was beautiful, too. I can't exactly explain how she was beautiful. She was plump, and she didn't have movie star features. "Movie star beautiful" is the name Jeanné and I used for ladies who had perfect features and gorgeous hair.

I think the reason I thought Mrs. Fedora was beautiful was because she smiled a lot, and I liked the way her grey eyes crinkled at the corners. Her eyes *were* movie star beautiful. They were grey and fringed with curly dark eyelashes.

But something about the kind of lady she was made me love her right away. The moment we came in the door she made Mama and me feel like she would rather be spending time with us than doing any other thing in the world. She made us feel like her house was our house.

She had iced tea, cheese straws, and devil's food cake ready for us. We went into the kitchen while she took the ice out of the refrigerator and ran water over it so it would come out easily. She'd made the ice in the refrigerator. I thought it was amazing the Fedoras didn't have to buy ice by the block from Mr. Tolly's ice plant the way we did.

I was wondering where Frankie was. Mrs. Fedora must have read my thoughts.

"I apologize for Frankie. She'll be here any moment." She explained, "Her daddy took her out to see our new foal, born just this morning. I imagine Mr. Fedora's forgotten the time."

"You have horses?" I asked in awe.

"Just two." She laughed. Her laugh was like silver bells at Christmas. "Why, I should say three now, shouldn't I?"

My eyes must have shown how interested I was, because she said, "You know what I'm thinking? You and Frankie could go horseback riding some day."

I didn't know how to answer. I was happy and excited about the possibility, but I was a tiny bit afraid. I'd never ridden a horse.

When she passed praline candy I was pleased. I didn't think ordinary people made pralines. I thought a person could only buy that kind of candy at a store in New Orleans. Now here was Mama's new friend, Miss Frances, saying she'd made the candy herself. She promised to give me the recipe. Not Mama. *Me.* I decided this was an unusual person, a lady who could make a twelve-year-old feel this special herself.

We heard a man's voice out back saying, "I'll see you later, Princess," and Frankie came into the room. At first I could only see the strange, abnormal mouth. Her lip was ugly. I quickly shifted my glance to her eyes. They were exactly like her mother's. Her skin was white and looked like the skin of the porcelain doll I'd seen at Gayfer's Department Store in Mobile.

Her eyes smiled at me, but her hand quickly went to her mouth to hide the smile there. At that moment I knew I was going to be Frankie Fedora's friend forever. I was glad my mama had prepared me for Frankie's affliction. I had a flash of memory about the times I had judged people for the way they looked, but I don't think I liked her because of guilt. I would have loved Frankie, no matter what.

She sat in the living room and had iced tea with us. I wouldn't look at her mouth. We both felt shy. Mama and Miss Frances were talking like crazy. I knew Mama felt the way I did about Mrs. Fedora. They liked talking with one another about everything, especially all the latest books.

Frankie said, "Wanna go to my room?"

She spoke in a somewhat muffled voice, but her words weren't difficult to understand. I was glad to be away from the talk of books that were too old for me to understand, and I think Frankie was, too.

Frankie's room was prettier than any I had ever seen. There was a canopy over the bed. The bedspread and the canopy had tiny sprigs of pink roses all over. The walls were painted the same pale pink of the roses.

But my reason for liking Frankie had nothing to do with her nice mother, or her house, or the refrigerator, or even the fact she had a problem. I felt bad for her, but I didn't pity her. She had that same way her mother had of making a person feel . . . unique. That word came back to me from our vocabulary lesson in fourth grade. I remembered the synonyms, too. Uncommon. Special. Unusual. Exceptional.

Once we got started, we talked as much as Mama and Miss Frances. We, too, had read the same books. We both liked seeing school plays, and being outdoors, and flowers. She'd never been blackberry picking. I promised to take her.

50

Before I knew it she was asking me to come over someday soon to go horseback riding with her, and I was asking her to come to my house so Papa could take us crabbing.

"You're just gonna love the bay," I said, "but your skin's so fair, you'd better take a big hat."

Self-consciously she covered her lip. I wanted to tell her, "I don't care about your lip. I won't ever look at it if it bothers you," but I couldn't tell her that. Maybe later.

When I told her I'd seen a fifty-five-foot monster in the bayou she didn't doubt me at all. She was so excited she grabbed my hand and made me promise I'd show it to her.

When Miss Frances drove us home Mama asked her and Frankie to come in for a spell.

"Thank you," Miss Frances said, "but not this time. I know you have supper to fix for your family. But I'd love to come visit with y'all another time."

I felt suddenly shy. As we got out of the car I said, my voice soft and timid, "Don't forget to bring Frankie with you when you come."

For some reason, that made Mama and Miss Frances laugh. Frankie was laughing, too. She waved at me until their car was out of sight. I waved back, my heart filled with hopeful pleasure.

I'm glad I didn't know then of all the difficulty in store for us.

Rumor Spreader

August was a wonderful month for me. Frankie and I became good friends. Jeanné was jealous at first, but she soon enjoyed Frankie, too.

Papa took all three of us crabbing. Frankie wore a big straw hat. Just to be sure she didn't feel foolish, Jeanné and I wore hats, too. There was a lot of giggling and silliness when a stiff breeze came up. The wind kept us frantically grabbing at our hats to keep them from wafting into the bay.

Frankie thought it funny that I called my father "Papa," and I thought she was funny when I'd hear her say her "daddy" did this, her "daddy" did that. I could tell she was as proud of her daddy as I was proud of my papa.

Jeanné and I realized we didn't argue as much when we were with Frankie. We weren't exactly sure why, but maybe it was because Frankie had learned to live with a big problem.

Mama said that our knowing Frankie caused Jeanné and me to be more considerate. She said she'd noticed that trials and difficulties make some folks kinder and more understanding, and it sort of "rubs off" on people who know them.

"But other folks," she said, "get mean and hateful."

Jeanné and I figured Tom Henson must have had an entire bayou, or a bay, or a gulf of problems in his life, because something happened with Frankie and him that made us worry about his sanity.

One afternoon, when Frankie came to visit, the spectators were out in full force on the bayou across from our house. Naturally, Frankie wanted to know what was going on, so I said it was because of the sea monster. Her eyes lit up with excitement.

"I hope I get to see him," she said.

I asked Mama if we could go to the wharf for a while. Because of Frankie she said yes, but she quickly added, "Be careful."

We skirted the big magnolia tree in our front yard. I suspected Frankie wouldn't want people staring at her, and we could avoid the larger crowd by going behind the tree. I knew she wanted people to get to know her gradually. School was only a month away, and that seemed soon enough.

We went through Papa's shop to the wharf.

"We just wanna watch for a little while," I told Papa. "Frankie wants to see what the monster looks like."

"Have you seen him?" she asked Papa.

"Not yet, honey," he said. "Been too busy, but Marcie says he's quite a monster."

I don't know how I could tell, but I realized Papa still didn't believe in our monster. I sighed.

Papa asked Raymie to go out on the wharf with us. He chuckled, "We don't want our visitor to fall in the bayou, you know."

Out on the wharf I asked Raymie if he'd seen the monster that day. He shook his head no.

"Isn't this the wildest thing you've ever seen?" he asked, nodding toward the watching crowd. "They're slowing up a bit now, but just like Papa said he'd do, Tom Henson tole everybody in town and then some."

An old Ford truck drove up, chugging and rattling to a stop.

"Well, look at who just pulled up," Raymie said, gesturing toward the truck.

Tom Henson got out. He had a friend with him, and he was excitedly moving his arms and his mouth at a fast pace. He walked up the slanted board ramp to our wharf as if he owned the place. He didn't bother to ask permission, or say, "Excuse me," or anything polite people would have said.

"Y'all seen him today?" he asked Raymie.

"Nah," Raymie said, "haven't had time."

Tom, puffed up all full of himself, blustered, "I was just telling my friend here, he's from Grand Bay, I was telling him all about this here monster. I was explaining how things like this happen 'cause some evil person has cast a spell. Ain't that right, Raymie?"

I knew Raymie didn't believe that, but Tom was older than he, and I'm sure he knew Tom would be angry with anyone who disagreed with him.

Raymie mumbled, "I dunno."

"Well, you better, kid. You gonna find yourself in a peck of trouble if you don't know about such things. Stupid folks don't get nowhere in this world."

That really got my blood to boiling. I didn't like this rumor spreader talking to my brother that way.

"I don't think anyone put a spell on the bayou," I said. "I—I suppose sea monsters are probably like—like whales and stuff. You know, just a big fish—or—or—serpent."

Tom Henson spun around and stared at me. His yellow-green eyes gleamed. The corners of his narrow lips turned down before he spat out, "Whatta you know about it, girl? You're just a kid. You ain't ole enough to know *nothin'*."

I felt hurt. I had never known people who were deliberately hateful to others. I was blessed to be in two kind families—my own and my church family. I didn't want Frankie to have anything to do with this nasty, horrible man.

"Come on, Frankie," I said, taking her hand. "Let's go ask Papa if we can have a Coke."

Tom blocked our way. He snickered and said, "Sounds like you got some of Miss Helene's feisty ways, Miss Marcie. Well, maybe that's all right when you're growed up, but you're just a dirty little kid now."

Now Raymie was angry. His hand formed a fist at his side.

"Raymie," I whispered, "please, don't."

At that moment Tom noticed Frankie. He put his hand on her arm and looked at her.

"Who's this? What's wrong with your lip, kid?"

I'd never known anyone to be so unfeeling. I felt as if my heart were going to break for Frankie.

At that moment Papa came out on the wharf. Tom Henson stood for a moment, staring at him. I think he was something of a coward, because Papa's coming out made him back down. But even so, he shifted his gaze to Frankie's mouth. There was a nasty sneer on his face.

He gave Papa a brief nod, muttered "Hullo, Mr. Isaac" and turned to his friend from Grand Bay.

"C'mon, Pete," he growled. "Let's get outta here."

I was relieved when they turned to go. But when he reached the bottom of the wharf he turned and shrieked, "I know who cast that spell. They ain't no doubt who the evil one is, 'cause she's standing right there by you, Miss Marcie Delchamps."

Papa was too shocked to react. He stared at Tom with unbelieving eyes.

"What? What?" he asked.

I was relieved Raymie and Tom hadn't gotten in a fight. I was aching for Frankie, but I knew that Tom was wrong about her. *I* knew who the evil person was.

And it wasn't Frankie.

Hate Mongers

We walked from the wharf into the shop. Papa pulled two small Cokes out of his red Coca Cola icebox and handed them to us.

"You want one, too?" he asked Raymie.

Raymie was in a daze.

"Thanks, no," he mumbled.

He picked up a broom and began to sweep the floor fiercely. His hand was trembling; he was trying to control his anger.

Papa went behind the counter. He leaned over and looked at us, puzzled.

"What was that all about?" he asked.

Between Raymie and me, we told the entire story, carefully skipping the part about Frankie's lip. But Frankie herself surprised Raymie and me by telling Papa, "He wanted to know about my lip."

She said this as if it were a fact, nothing to be surprised about. There was no bitterness in her voice.

Papa's face revealed the shock he felt. He moved to the door in anger and looked out at the group standing there. His hand curled into a fist, too, the way Raymie's had.

"Why, that . . ." he began, but he stopped.

"It's all right, Mr. Isaac," Frankie said. "My mom says people like that are kinda sick in the head. She said folks like him have a bigger problem than I have. I didn't used to know what she meant, but now I'm eleven, I do." She paused, but when she added, "I mean, I almost do," her voice was a whisper.

Frankie's manner made each of us ashamed at the bad feelings we shared, even though we knew Tom Henson deserved our unkind thoughts. Her whispered, "almost do," made us know the hurt was there, but we had a lot to learn from Frankie about how to forgive and understand. We would all have a lot more to forgive in the next few weeks.

Jeanné told me about the first hint of trouble. On Monday of that week she came over in the morning to spend the day with me. We played jacks for a while, and then we drew pictures. A fierce rain was coming down. The rumble of thunder, with sudden flashes of lightning, made me restless.

We were lying on our stomachs on the floor, coloring. Jeanné was unusually quiet; something was bothering her. I stopped coloring and looked at her.

She stopped coloring, too. She must have felt me staring at her with this confused, puzzled expression. She sat up, sitting crossways on her legs, her arms folded.

In a quiet, unsure voice, she murmured, "I have to tell you something, but I'm afraid it's just gonna kill Miss Helene. And—and you're gonna be real mad, too."

I sat up. I pushed the crayons and paper away. I could feel disaster, ready to pierce my heart.

"What?" I asked. My voice broke.

She took a deep breath and said, "Tom Henson is telling folks that Frankie is evil. He says her family's moving here from New Orleans has caused the monster of the bayou to come."

My heart seemed to swell with alarm.

"Oh, no," I whispered. "No, he wouldn't do that."

"Well, he *did*," Jeanné said. "He *is*."

"But folks don't believe him, do they?"

"Some do," Jeanné said. "I don't know how many."

"Why, that's awful," I cried. "My mama and Miss Frances planned for us to get to know Frankie before school started. They thought if we got to know how nice she is, we wouldn't judge her by the way her mouth looks."

Jeanné shook her head sadly. "Yeah. It's the truth, too, isn't it? Once you get to know Frankie, you forget about how—how—ugly her lip is, don't you?"

We looked at one another for a long moment. Tears came to my eyes. I looked away and wiped them off with the back of my hand. When I looked back at Jeanné her eyes were wet, too.

Jeanné said, "Couldn't you just tell everyone there isn't a monster?"

I couldn't believe Jeanné still doubted me. I protested, "I can't say that, 'cause the monster is true."

Jeanné sighed. We didn't say anything for a long while. Finally, I stood up.

"Let's tell Mama," I said.

Mama was distressed. At first, she didn't know what to do, but after a bit her eyes lit up.

"Reverend Landry can preach a sermon about this at church. And maybe we'll call the Methodist preacher, too. We'll try to get thinking people on our side, folks who have some sense, and are kind."

"My mama will tell Father Le Clercq," Jeanné volunteered.

"Good," Mama said.

I reminded them, "A lot of folks don't go to church. What're we gonna do to be sure everyone knows Tom's just making things up?"

"I don't know for certain," Mama said, "but if we have enough people who know what Tom's doing, it's bound to be of some help."

Soon Mama was on the telephone, talking to Brother Landry and the Methodist preacher. And she called Jeanné's mama to have her tell Father Le Clercq, too.

The hardest call she had to make was to Miss Frances. She wanted her to be prepared, and she wanted them to know we were all willing to fight for Frankie.

But this was only Monday. Brother Landry said he could talk to some of the folks who went to prayer meeting on Wednesday night, but he wanted to make this message a part of a Sunday sermon.

"I don't think I'll have to mention the little girl's name," he said. "I'll just have a sermon about the harm judging can cause."

Everywhere we went that week, people were talking about Frankie and the curse of the bayou. When Raymie took Jeanné and me swimming at Willow Creek, a boy from my class at school came up to us as we sat on the bank of the creek, swinging our legs in the water.

"Hey, Marcie, I hear your new friend's got a bad problem," he said. "I hear she caused that dragon to come to be in the bayou."

"That's not true!" Jeanné and I both yelled at once.

Ordinarily we would have hooked the little fingers of our right hands and said the silly jingle we did when we said the same words at the same time. I would have said, "Pins," and she'd have said, "Needles." I would have asked, "What goes up the chimney?" and she would have answered, "Smoke." But this time we were too upset about our friend.

I said, "If you knew her, Joe Joe, you never would say such a thing."

Joe Joe's eyes narrowed and he said, "My mama saw that little harelip with her mama down to the grocery store. She said it's awful looking. She said it's not normal for a baby to be born with a lip like that. She knows for a fact that the mama must have been evil, maybe had a curse on her 'fore the baby was born. My daddy read an article in the newspaper that said that."

"Well, that's the craziest thing I ever heard in my whole, entire life, Joe Joe," Jeanné flared up.

And I said, "Yeah! It's *stupid*!"

"Why is it stupid?" he asked, wide-eyed.

He was serious. I wanted to say something wise and smart, but I had always believed that anything a person read in the newspaper had to be true. A seed of doubt was sewn in my mind.

"It's just stupid," I said again, but I wasn't as sure as I had been.

Joe Joe went on, enjoying the gossip. "My daddy said there's probably a lot more bad things gonna happen if the Fedoras don't move." He gave his head an emphatic shake. "And Tom Henson said if they don't decide to do it on their own, he's gonna make things so bad they'll have to go."

"Why, he's just a mean, hateful blockhead," I cried. I couldn't believe I was hearing these unfair words.

"You better shut up," Jeanné said to him. Our mamas had taught us *never* to say shut up to anyone. That was the very worst of bad man-

ners, but I decided this was one time Jeanné had a right to say it.

George Fosell heard our conversation above the noise of the splashing and yelling in the creek. He came over to us and gave me a poke in my back.

In a singsong voice, he taunted, "Marcie's friend's a bunny, Marcie's friend's a bunny." He gave a high, malicious laugh. "Heh, heh, heh. You're probably evil, too, Miss Marcie Parcie, if you have a evil friend like that."

I jumped up, furious, confused, and hurt. Jeanné was on her feet as quickly as I. I grabbed my towel from where it hung on a tree limb.

"Let's go, Jeanné," I said. "I don't wanna have anything to do with rumor spreaders and hate mongers." I was remembering Papa's words.

I rushed up the banks and started through the woods, thoroughly distressed. Jeanné yanked her towel from the tree and was close behind me.

As we left, several of the boys took up the chant. "Marcie's friend's a bunny, Marcie's friend's a bunny."

In our frustration we forgot to tell Raymie we were leaving. From across the creek we heard him holler, "Marcie! Jeanné! Where do you think you're going?"

"Home!" I choked out.

In a moment Raymie was swimming across the creek. On our side he jumped onto the grassy bank and charged after us. He grabbed my arm.

"What happened?" he asked, baffled at the sight of our angry, tear-streaked faces.

In my efforts to stop my crying I could scarcely talk. In a tangled jumble of anger and hurt I told him of Joe Joe, and George, and the other boys. Jeanné helped out.

Raymie may have been a tease, but ever since we'd been in that storm together on the shrimp boat in the Gulf, he'd been protective of me.

"Y'all get on home!" he commanded. "I'll take care of those cowards."

I didn't want to leave now. I wondered what Raymie would do. His friend, Hank, was at the creek, too. I was afraid they'd get in a big fight, but my brother gave me a gentle push.

"Go on, home, honey," he said.

Raymie never called me honey. My throat ached from held-back tears. At first the wish to cry came from the unfair words about Frankie. Now they came from the tender sweetness of my gruff, teasing brother.

Jeanné and I ran, gripping one another's hands tightly. We ran down the street that led into town, across the Grand Pont, the big bridge that crossed the bayou before St. Bridget's church.

I don't know how far we ran, but Jeanné finally pulled at my hand and said, "Marcie, my side is hurting bad. Let's stop."

I stopped. I was breathing hard, and my side hurt, too.

"Joe Joe's a mean, hateful nookie nark," she said.

Catching my breath, I asked, "What's a nookie nark?"

"I don't know, but he is one," she said.

We began to giggle at the silly, made-up name, but the giggle became an odd mingle of laughter and tears that made us weak. By the side of the road we held on to one another, laughing and crying. When we finally stopped, we walked the rest of the way to my house, quiet now, scarcely speaking.

Mama and Papa had protected me. Before I met Tom Henson, I hadn't known any mean people who said cruel untruths. The people I had known in my church and school cared about me, and I cared about them. I had never known anyone close to me with a problem like Frankie's. I was afraid for her. The people in our town weren't unkind, but Tom's stories had turned their minds against her.

As soon as we had a chance to talk with Mama I decided I'd invite Frankie over to visit me. I'd make it up to her if I possibly could, but I had no idea how I'd be able to.

Oh, please, I prayed, *help Frankie to be all right.*

Storm Warnings

We found Mama in the kitchen, snapping green beans. When she saw our faces she sat us down and poured us glasses of iced tea. Then she listened as we told her what Joe Joe had said.

Mama said that what Joe Joe's daddy said wasn't true. "Sometimes," she said, "when people aren't educated about life, they believe foolish and ridiculous myths that don't have a speck of truth in them."

She told us that a person who had physical impairments wasn't being punished for having an evil mother. She reminded us about the Bible story where the disciples asked Jesus whether a man was blind because he or his parents sinned. Jesus said neither one of them had sinned, but the man was born blind so that Jesus could heal the man and glorify God.

"Maybe Jesus will heal Frankie too!" I said.

"Maybe he will," Mama said. "But, Marcie, Frankie already glorifies God with the way she handles her affliction."

I nodded. Mama was right.

Then Jeanné thought of something else. "But how come the *newspaper* lied?" she asked.

Mama laughed. "Well, your favorite movie star, Will Rogers, said you can't believe everything you read in the papers.

"And what's more important," she went on, "is that another great man said that, too. And he said we never believe gossip about others unless the gossip is proven to be true."

"What man was that?" I asked.

She grinned as she answered, "Your own papa."

My spirits perked up. That made me feel better.

After Jeanné left, I asked Mama if Frankie could come over to visit on Thursday.

Mama said, "I'm afraid not, Marcie. Papa and I are going to Pascagoula on Thursday."

I was worried about Frankie. I wanted to see her right away. "Please, Mama?" I begged. "Mr. Jake and Raymie could watch over us. Please?"

Mama smiled. Mama and Papa often teased me about being stubborn when I wanted something badly enough. I didn't have to beg too long this time, though. Maybe she didn't feel like arguing with me, or maybe she realized having Frankie here would be all right with Mr. Jake and Raymie. Whatever the reason, she quickly agreed.

On Wednesday night she said, "We're leaving early in the morning. You probably won't even be up yet, but Mr. Jake said you should be sure to tell him or Raymie if you and Frankie go anywhere at all, Marcie. And, honey, I'd like to suggest you don't go down to the stores or any place where someone might hurt Frankie's feelings. We have to be sure this gossip has died down before we expose her to such unthinking judgments."

"Yes, ma'am," I said. I wasn't worried. Frankie and I would have a good time. We could draw, and we could play jacks, or dominoes, or marbles. And there were a lot of blackberries growing in the field next to our house. They would be fun to pick if it didn't rain.

"What time is Frankie coming, Mama?" I asked.

"Her daddy's dropping her off about nine in the morning," Mama said. And then she added, "Whatever you do, don't go down to the wharf. The monster seekers aren't as eager now, but I don't want y'all to run into Tom Henson or any of his friends."

She didn't have to worry about that. I'd been thinking about the bayou monster a lot. Actually, I couldn't seem to get him off my mind, even with all the fun things I'd been doing. Mama had told me to stay away from the wharf and the oak. After our experience with Tom

Henson I'd been happy to obey. Sometimes I wished I'd never seen that monster.

On Thursday morning I was up before Mama and Papa left. There was no rain, but the clouds were dark and threatening.

Papa was saying to Mama, "I'll swear, Pet, if I didn't know any better I'd say we were in for a storm."

"Maybe we shouldn't go," she suggested.

"Ahh, it's all right. I haven't heard anything on the radio, and the storm warnings aren't up. I called the weatherman in Mobile. He says it doesn't look bad. He says there seems to be a hurricane forming off the Texas coast, but it doesn't seem to be coming this way. We'll probably get a bit of rain."

He sighed. "I hate to drive in it, but I just have to pick up that trawling net I promised Billy Jim Boisonot. He wants to go out shrimping by next Tuesday. We need to give ourselves time to tar it first."

Mama patted Papa's cheek and said, "That's what I like about you, Isaac Delchamps. You take care of your customers."

When they drove away I felt a strange twinge in my stomach. I didn't know what caused the feeling. Was it fear? For Mama and Papa? For Frankie and me? Was this a forewarning that something bad was going to happen? I shook my head to clear away the threatening thoughts.

Soon I was cooking breakfast for Mr. Jake and Raymie, looking forward to the time with Frankie. Mr. Jake had told Papa he'd help Raymie at the shop for the day.

Raymie teased me about the way I'd cooked the eggs.

"Once-over-light means just what it says, shrimp. You're not supposed to break the yolk and curl the edges."

My Cajun friend took up for me, as usual.

"Miss Marcie, she maybe need to learn about eggs, but she much much good at frying de fish, huh?" he said.

Raymie had taught me to fry fish when we'd gone on that shrimping trip in the Gulf.

"Yeah," he said, wavering his hand to mean so-so. "She's a pretty good fish cooker, I guess."

I didn't mind his teasing. I didn't even mind washing and drying the dishes when they had gone down to the shop. I couldn't stop glancing at the kitchen clock above the sink. Seven-thirty. I could scarcely wait until nine o'clock.

There was a light rain falling when they finally arrived. Mr. Fedora came to the door with Frankie. He was holding his umbrella over her head.

"Been trying to rain all night," he said. "Big, black clouds over to the east. Well, you girls won't mind staying home, will you?"

"We don't care if it rains forever," I said. "We have lots of things to do right here in the house."

"Uh huh!" Frankie said.

We both giggled. I don't know what there was about Frankie, but when we were together the slightest word or happening could start us giggling.

Mr. Fedora started down the porch steps, but he came back to hug Frankie. "Now y'all stay outta this weather, you hear?" he said.

"We'll be good, Daddy. Bye," Frankie said through her giggles. "See you after the storm . . ." She stopped and mischievously added, ". . . sugar."

We laughed together. Mr. Fedora went down the steps, shaking his head. He was still laughing as he drove away.

The rain continued all morning. I went out on the front porch to look. I was surprised to see the water was only a few feet below our wharf. I hadn't realized there had been enough rain to cause the water level to rise that high.

At noon the rain almost stopped. There were low, thunderous clouds, but there was only a spitting rainfall.

"Let's go down to the shop and see Raymie," I suggested.

Mama had made a mess of turnip greens and ham. Frankie had helped me make corn bread and a cucumber and tomato salad.

Of course there were no monster watchers. In fact, there were no people outside at all. No cars, either. And no boats on the bayou.

Raymie and Mr. Jake were glad to see us. No customers had come in all morning. They were bored.

"Y'all wanna come up for dinner?" I asked. "It's ready."

"Why don't you go on up first, Raymie?" Mr. Jake suggested, but Raymie said, "You know what I think, Mr. Jake? Nobody's gonna be coming out in this rain. Why don't we both go up together? We'll put a note on the door."

Raymie and Mr. Jake closed the shop, and the four of us went back to the house. We ate, and during lunch Mr. Jake told funny stories about his days as a boy in Houma, Louisiana.

After lunch Mr. Jake suggested Raymie stay up at the house. He said there wouldn't be any business, unless someone might want a screw driver, or a lug wrench, or some tool like that.

"Oooh, goody," I said. "Raymie, would you take us for a drive around the coast to see how high the bay has risen?"

He liked the idea. So Raymie, Frankie, and I piled into Raymie's decrepit old Buick and set out.

"Around the coast" was the phrase we used to describe the way the bayou curved along the land and blended into Portersville Bay. On hot summer nights Papa would drive us "around the coast" to cool us off.

After we rounded the curve leading from the bayou to the bay, there weren't many shacks. In fact, there were no businesses and only a few homes. Folks from Mobile had a few small, screened-porch cottages. But there were several large summer homes scattered along the coast. These were square, two-storied, and white. The one closest to the bay was the Slade house, owned by a doctor who lived in Montgomery. He'd come to our church a few times that summer.

We put-putted along; Raymie's car wasn't in very good condition. He'd bought it a couple of years ago with thirty-five dollars he'd made on a shrimping trip.

There's something thrilling about a storm. Even though we didn't know how big this storm was going to be, we sensed something mysterious in the air. When we had driven past the shacks, the ice plants, the seafood factories, and the shipyard, we came to that place where the two bodies of water meet.

At the union of the two waters a definite color change could usually be seen. The dark waters of the bayou became the wide, beige waters of the bay. But today the bay was dark, too. A dark, gun-metal grey. The waves rushed up to the shore with a fierceness seldom seen on our calm bay.

Frankie and I pressed our noses against the windows, drinking in the scene. As we passed Rosie's Fresh Fish House, Raymie turned around to look.

"You know," he said, "I think Rosie has a storm warning flag up."

He drove along, looking out at the bay, wondering. After a bit he tossed his head and said, "Aww, that's probably just for boats. I don't think we're gonna have a hurricane or anything."

That word, *hurricane*, made a chill run down my back. I'd never been in a real hurricane, but they had often come close to us. We'd read in the papers about all the deaths and destruction that hurricanes caused.

"This isn't a hurricane, I can tell," I said.

But what did I know?

Shelter
at the Slade House

Just past Rosie's place we turned off the coast road onto a narrow shell lane. The lane went to the end of a small peninsula that jutted out into the bay. There were huge blocks of cement all over the tip of the land. A cement building of some sort had once been there. Now there were only broken blocks with their twisted and rusted rods.

Raymie parked the car, and we climbed on the boulders, laughing. The wind had become wild, and we could barely keep our balance. A few times I almost slipped and fell on the rusty rods.

"Get back in the car!" Raymie yelled over the noise of the howling wind.

Suddenly it began to rain hard, the water coming down in silver waves. We ran for the car. As Frankie and I settled into the front seat, giggling and hooting, Raymie put the key in the ignition and turned it. Nothing. He grabbed at the choke and pulled, but the engine sputtered, choked, spit, and finally died altogether.

"Oh, golly," Raymie moaned. "The battery."

Raymie put his head down on the wheel and sighed.

"Hey, folks!" I cried. "Ain't this fun?"

"Yeah!" Frankie agreed. She was enjoying the fierceness of the wind and rain as much as I.

She said, "We can play word games in the car while we're waiting for the storm to stop."

Raymie raised his head. I could tell by the expression on his face he didn't think this was fun at all. He sighed again. The sigh seemed to come from his toes.

"I musta been crazy mad to think I could take y'all for a ride on a day like this. Papa'd die if he knew I was so stupid."

"It's okay, Raymie," I tried to assure him, but I began to realize there was something eerie about this rain. The sight of Raymie's slumped shoulders frightened me.

Raymie sat up suddenly, taking charge. "Now, you two listen to me. We're gonna go up to the Slade house. You're gonna have to hold on to me with all your strength. You, too, Frankie. And once I get y'all settled, I'm gonna get back to Rosie's and make a telephone call to Hank to come help me start the car. Okay?"

"Why don't you use Dr. Slade's phone?" I asked.

"I think they've left for the summer, and they don't keep their phone hooked up all year," Raymie replied.

"I don't wanna get out in that rain," I said, meaning it.

"I'm sorry," he said, "but you don't have a choice. Look over there at the way the water is almost covering the land. This entire little peninsula may be covered with water before Hank and I can get back. We have to go."

I looked where he pointed. And then I understood why Raymie looked so worried.

The wind was so strong now we had trouble getting out of the car. With all the strength he could muster, Raymie opened the doors. We could scarcely stand, but he clasped his strong arms around us on either side. Our hands grasped him tightly, and we started back up the narrow shell lane to the coast road where we had entered.

At the beginning of the peninsula road we turned right toward the summer homes. The water had risen to the middle of the road now. We sloshed through it and across the soaked grass to the Slade house.

When we reached the screened door on the front porch Raymie screamed as loudly as he could, "Anybody home? Hey! Anybody here?"

There was no answer. The clouds were low and menacing now, making the afternoon dark; if anyone were here there would probably be a light on somewhere in the house. There was no light to be seen.

The house, as large as it was, was on two-foot pilings. Latticework covered the pilings to make the house more attractive. Behind the steps there was an opening in the latticework. Raymie pushed Frankie and me behind this.

"Wait here," he yelled. "I'm gonna see if I can get y'all into the house."

I didn't want him to go. Frankie and I crouched together in the dirt, clinging to one another. We were afraid to let go of one another, afraid we'd blow away. We didn't even try to talk.

As we waited we were both aware of a strange sound. All of the birds of the bay and the countryside were screeching and crying. These weren't birdcalls or joyful early morning chirpings. These were hideous, screeching sounds. We covered our ears.

Time seemed to have stopped and waited, holding its breath. Only minutes had passed since Raymie had left, but we felt we had been crouched behind those steps forever.

At last Raymie appeared. "I can get you in," he yelled, speaking above the din of wind and rain and birds.

He had found a torn place in a porch screen and lifted it. He was surprised to find a window on the porch that opened easily into the living room.

Relieved to find shelter, we sank to the floor, not wanting to sit on the cushions of the wicker furniture in our wet clothes.

"Raymie," I said. "We're trespassing. The Slades are gonna be mad with us."

I'd been in trouble with Mama and Papa about trespassing a few times in the last year.

"Marcie," Raymie said, "there isn't anyone in the world who would expect you to stay outside in a storm like this."

He went to try the phone in the kitchen to see if it was working. Disappointed, he came back to us. For a long moment he looked at us, chewing his lip in concern. His eyes scanned the big windows that were all around the house. I knew what he was thinking. He was afraid to leave us alone, and he hated going into the storm again.

He made up his mind. "Now, listen, you two. Y'all are gonna be all right. Don't even think of going outside of this house for any reason."

I wailed, "You're liable to drown out there. The water's gonna be covering the road pretty soon. Your car's probably already covered."

"I hope not," he said, "but I have to do it. I'll be careful."

He said the peninsula was a bit higher than the land here, so maybe his car would be all right. Then he tried to make us feel better by saying, "Listen. This house is sturdy, and I can't risk walking you home. Too dangerous."

81

Even sturdy houses are swept off their foundations sometimes, I thought, but I didn't say it out loud.

"This is the best place for you to be in a hurricane," Raymie said.

That was the first time the word seemed to hold truth.

"A *hurricane*!" I gasped. "Is this a hurricane?"

Frankie's hand went to her mouth in fear. Her face paled.

"A hurricane," she whispered.

I could see Raymie was sorry he'd said that word, but it was too late now. We knew the worst.

He tried to cover his words by saying, "Well, it's probably not a hurricane, but it's the worst storm I've seen since the hurricane I was in when I was seven."

I shuddered. I didn't remember being in that hurricane. I was only four then, but I remembered Mama, and Papa, and Raymie, too, talking about the hurricane of 1926. We'd lived in a smaller house than the one we lived in now, and we'd had to go to the school for safety.

"Please don't leave us, Raymie," I begged, but he had made up his mind.

He said, "Have to. If I can get Hank to rev up my battery we can get you girls over to Frankie's house. It's further away from the water, it's on a slight rise, and it's brick. Frankie, I'll call your mama to let her know y'all are all right, and I'll have to take a little while to board up the windows at our house, Marcie. But I'll come as soon as possible. You'll be all right."

I didn't believe we were all right. I wanted him to stay or let us go with him, but I knew, with the wind becoming stronger every moment, that Frankie and I could never stand against it.

In fact, the sounds of the storm were growing increasingly sinister. There were sudden, horrible crashes, the sounds of possible breaking glass, snapping and falling trees. Added to these uncertain sounds were the continuous howling of the winds and the pounding of the surf.

Raymie stood at the door a long time before he opened it. In an effort at sounding casual he spoke in a strange, gruff voice.

"Listen you two. Don't be worried. I'll be back soon, you hear?"

He left.

Frankie and I didn't speak for a long time. We stood pressing ourselves against the windows, trying to watch him across the porch and through the screened windows, but he was quickly out of sight.

The storm had caused the world to be as dark as dusk. I decided to turn on a few lights. Maybe that would cheer us up.

But the lights wouldn't go on. Because of the storm, of course. Worst of all, we had no idea where we could find a candle in this strange house.

Eye of the Storm

The knowledge that darkness would soon be upon us spurred us into action. We began to go through every drawer in the house, looking for candles and matches. We searched the dining room buffet drawers, the drawers to the little side tables in the living room, the built-in book and china shelves.

There wasn't a candle to be found.

"Let's try the kitchen," I said. "There are probably matches there, and, who knows, maybe we'll find candles, too."

We found matches, but there were no candles.

There was a small room off the kitchen. We went into the room listlessly. We had just about given up, but in a closed cupboard down below I found a box way in the back. I was so sure we wouldn't find anything that I almost didn't open it. But Frankie grabbed at the box and said,

"Marcie. Look what's written on it. *Christmas candles.*"

We were so excited we opened the package with shaking hands. Most of the candles were melted into strange shapes, but we picked out eight that were still good. In the dining room buffet, we found some candleholders. We took the candles and holders into the living room, placed them on the table in front of the couch, and lit two of them. The yellow petals of flame raised our spirits.

We tried to cheer each other up. We told jokes and riddles. We played clapping games. And word games. But after a long time we ran out of words and ideas. We sat, silently thinking our own worried thoughts.

After a while I asked Frankie, "What are you thinking about?"

Without hesitating, she said, "My mother and daddy. I know they're so worried about me. I feel bad 'cause I begged them to let me go to your house. If I hadn't come, we'd both be safe in our homes by now."

"No," I said. "It's my fault. I asked Raymie to take us for a ride."

I swallowed to keep my voice from showing how close to tears I was. "I'm worried about my folks, too. The storm is probably worse at Pascagoula. Pascagoula's right off the Gulf. And I'm worried about Raymie."

I wanted to cry, but I knew that wasn't the thing to do right now. I think we were each trying to be brave for the other.

"I know," Frankie said. She sounded as if she'd like to cry, too. "I been praying both our families are all right."

"Me, too," I said. "I've been praying, too."

We were quiet for a long time then. I was sure the little peninsula would be covered by now. Raymie's car would be under water. When I peered out the window I noticed the bay had crossed the road and was creeping up the lawn toward the house.

About four in the afternoon the rain stopped. The wind was still. There was no sound at all. The silence was unnatural and eerie. Moments before, the wind and rain sounds had been dreadful; shutters hammering against windows, the continued snapping and falling of trees, and branches thrown against the house by the wrathful wind.

I could hear my own breathing in the spooky quietness.

I put my hand on Frankie's arm and said, "Something weird is happening."

We both stood and moved to the window where we had come in. We crawled through the torn screen, out to the veranda.

We gasped in wonder. The sky was a bright yellow-green. The water, clear and steel grey now, and almost calm, reflected the yellow in small cups. There was no sound whatsoever.

"Oh, my goodness. It's stopped," Frankie whispered. "Now the water will go down and Raymie will come for us."

I wanted to believe that was true, but I remembered folks talking about hurricanes. I'd heard them saying there was a time when this stillness would happen. We might even be in the eye of the hurricane. If that were true, the storm would come again with a fury more frenzied than before. We'd all be drowned.

I didn't say this to Frankie, but I think she knew. She'd lived in New Orleans. I suppose she had been in bad storms there.

We stood there, motionless, for a long time, frightened but dazed by the beauty of the water and the sky. I thought of how my papa, during a storm, would quote from the Bible, "The heavens declare the glory of God, and the firmament showeth his handiwork."

I wondered if I'd ever see Papa again.

Whispering, Frankie said, "Look. The water is up to the bottom step now."

"Yeah, let's go back in," I said. "Maybe we should go upstairs."

I remembered the older people in town talking about a tidal wave that swallowed all the homes on the Gulf. I wondered if that same wave had flooded the homes here on Portersville Bay. I decided to keep quiet about this story. Saying it might make it happen.

Again, we sat in the living room. We both wanted to go upstairs, feeling we'd be safer from the storm there, but a fear of the dark, unknown second story kept us from going up. We sat on the floor, cross-legged, in front of the low tables where our two candles flickered. We looked about the room at the weird shadows being cast on the walls by the wicker furniture.

"If the water starts coming in," I said, "all the Slade's furniture and nice things are gonna be ruined. Maybe we could save some of it."

Frankie liked the idea. We started in, moving everything we could to higher places. Together, we picked up the small tables and placed them on the dining room tables. The furniture was mostly wicker, and not as heavy as furniture made of wood or steel, but still, we lifted items far too heavy for us. We grunted and heaved, panted and gasped. When we had done all we could do in the living room and dining room we went into the kitchen and began putting the china and silver-ware, pots and pans, table linens, everything we could take from the lower shelves, onto the counters and higher shelves.

By now the rooms were so dark we could no longer see without our candles. We lit a few and took them to the window to see how high the water had risen on the porch. We were shocked to see the grey boards of the porch were now covered with a few inches of water. Another two inches and the water would be in the living room.

Every so often, a flash of lightning would light up the bay. The bay now stretched from the horizon to the living room of this house.

"Frankie," I said, "I think we better go upstairs."

"Yeah, me, too," she nodded, awestruck at the sight of the water.

We decided we should see if we could find any food downstairs before we went to the upper floor; we were both hungry. We found a box of unopened soda crackers and a bottle of apple juice in the cupboard. We gathered all the candles, even the bent-out-of-shape ones, and the box of matches, and started up the stairs.

"Maybe we oughta just stop here on the landing," I suggested.

Frankie nodded her head in quick agreement. For some reason we didn't want to go into those upper rooms.

We crouched on the landing. Every so often, one of us would look up at the stairs anxiously.

The grandfather clock on the landing chimed seven o'clock. I couldn't believe it was only seven. Hours seemed to have passed since Raymie had gone. Usually, in August, the sun would be shining, and we would play until seven-thirty or eight. But the storm had wiped out the August light.

We sat there for a long time. The frightful sounds and the fear of unknown terrors made sleep impossible. We leaned against the step going up the stairs and tried to relax.

My eyes were closed. There were no thoughts circling in my head now. None at all. When Frankie spoke, I was startled.

"Marcie?" she asked. "Are you asleep?"

"No," I said, "but I wish I could. Maybe the time would go faster. Maybe we wouldn't even know if we drowned."

"Are you real scared?"

I started to say no, but there was something about this situation that made truth even more important than usual.

"Yeah." I exhaled. "Real scared."

"Me, too. Marcie, there's something I wanna ask you."

I nodded solemnly to let her know she could go ahead.

"Do you think I'm ugly?"

The question really shocked me. I sat up. My first reaction was not wanting to hurt her.

"Well—no. I—I think you're beautiful," I cried.

I was embarrassed then; had I really been truthful?

"You couldn't think that," she said. There was an edge of bitterness in her voice. "I know my mouth is ugly, so how can you say I'm beautiful?"

I knew she was being honest, but my good feelings for her bubbled to the top of any of the bad.

"Well," I said, taking a big breath, "I think you have the prettiest eyes I've ever seen on anyone. You and your mama, too."

"But my lip—my lip is so horrible," she said. Her eyes were fixed on mine. I knew only truth would do.

"It—it's not *horrible*," I said. "It's not normal, but . . ."

I wanted to say the right thing more than I ever had in my life. I wanted to make her feel all right, but I wanted to be honest.

I don't know what made me do what I did then. I reached over and touched her mouth, ever so gently, and I said, "I don't ever think about it, 'cause you're the nicest girl I ever knew, and I wish I could be just like you."

We had never been in a situation like this. We both began to cry. We put our arms around each other and sobbed. The fears we had held in all afternoon came pouring out. I don't know how long we cried.

This may seem hard to believe, but we actually slept for a short while, all curled up, on the landing of the Slade's summerhouse, during a hurricane.

An hour later, something awakened me. The storm noises were as loud and frightening as ever, but that didn't seem to be the reason I'd awakened. The house seemed strange. There was an odd, spooky feeling in the air. I rubbed my eyes and sat up to see our two candles were almost burned out. The wicks were flickering in the melted wax. Quickly, I lit two more candles, the tallest I could find. I reached to place them on a higher step.

That's when I saw the man.

I screamed. Frankie, awakened by my scream, leaped to a sitting position. And I stared in open-mouthed horror at Tom Henson, coming down the stairs toward us.

Water Moccasin

"Well, look at what the cat done drug in," Tom Henson drawled in his rude way. "I been peeking in on y'all. Whatcha trying to do with that furniture downstairs? Hoping you gonna get a reward from Dr. Slade?"

My mouth had gone completely dry. I couldn't work up enough moisture to reply. My heart was jumping around in my rib cage like it had gone crazy.

I looked at Frankie. There was no color in her face at all. Her eyes were big with fright.

Tom walked down and sat on the stairs a few steps above us, his hands on his knees. His mouth was twisted in a snarl as he stared at us.

"Well? What's wrong with you two stupid kids? Cat gotcha tongues?"

"No, sir," I managed to say. I swallowed, took a breath, and said, "Have you been here all afternoon?"

"Who do you think cut the screen and broke the door latch so y'all was able to get in? Did you think your dumb brother done figgered that out? Or did you think he was a magician?"

That struck him as funny, and for a few moments he screeched with laughter. But when a particularly loud crack of thunder shook the house, he flinched and put his head on the steps above, covering his eyes.

Why, he's more afraid than we are, I realized. Somehow his cowardice gave me hope. I figured a scary man couldn't be any more frightening than a hurricane.

"Did you come here to get away from the storm?" I asked. "Or did you come to steal from the Slades?"

"Well, ain't you the smarty girl?" he said. He paused, then he snapped, "None of your business!"

I was sorry I had been cocky. I had given him reason to be mean to Frankie. No telling what he may do to us now.

He leaned forward and looked at Frankie with glittering eyes.

He said, "You know what I think, kid? I think *you* caused this hurricane. We ain't had a hurricane here since 1926. Since you come to town we got a monster in the bayou and a hurricane. Probably the whole town gonna be wiped out, all because of you."

I forgot my fear. Tom Henson's cruel words made my blood boil.

I put my hands on my hips and yelled at him, "You're just a mean, hateful *worm!* My mama said you don't know what you're talking about; nobody cast a spell on Frankie's mama, and Frankie hasn't cast a spell on the bayou or anything else. And you can just shut up, and stop being mean to my friend!"

Frankie covered her mouth to hide her pleased smile. Tom Henson laughed at me, a high, girlish giggle. He couldn't seem to stop. He snorted and choked in a hysterical way.

He continued to sputter as he said, "Well, if you ain't the feisty one! Like I said before, you're just like Miss Helene. Humph! Your ma thinks she's so high and mighty. I remember just last spring when she had that memorial service for that silly ole Cajun and a little black nigra. She's so ignorant she don't know different folks shouldn't mix. Yeeh!"

That kind of unfair talk made me brave. I came closer to him, my foot on the step below him, my chin jutting out, close to his face. I hoped I looked as mean as he did.

I hollered as loudly as I could, "You better not say anything else about Mr. Jake, or my friend, Lissez, and especially my mama. Everybody knows what she did was right. And—and I was proud of her."

I felt Frankie's hand on my arm, pulling me back. I heard her murmuring, "No, Marcie," but I was ready to fight, and this new, brave me was a stranger I couldn't control.

Tom Henson's face twisted in an ugly grimace. He growled, "I don't have to put up with no disrespectful brat."

I knew I had gone too far. But I didn't want this hateful man, this man who had caused so much trouble in town, to hurt my friend any longer. And I wasn't going to have him saying bad things about folks I loved.

I sat back down on the landing beside Frankie, trembling.

An astounding crash of thunder actually shook the house. Tom fiercely uttered a few bad words and cowered against the wall of the stairway.

"When's this thing gonna end?" he asked the air around him.

Just to be spiteful, I said, "Probably never." I certainly hoped I was wrong, but I was disgusted with him. Why, a man who was almost thirty ought to be trying to protect *us*.

There was a crazed gleam in his eyes, and although I knew he was a yellowbelly coward, I continued to be afraid of what he might do. His wild eyes gave me chills. I knew cowards were sometimes more dangerous than any other people, especially when they were with people smaller and not as strong as they.

I tried to get hold of my fears by pretending I wasn't afraid. But when I held one of the candlesticks toward the bottom of the stairs my fears came back in full force.

"Frankie, look!" I gasped. "The water is in the house now. It—it's up to the front step."

We all leaned forward.

"Lemme have one of them candles," Tom Henson roared. He didn't wait for me to hand the candle to him. He snatched it off the step, out of its holder, and headed down the stairs with it.

I suppose he saw the water and realized there was no place to go, because he quickly wheeled around and came back up the stairs.

"We all gonna drown because of you, girl," he said, roughly grasping Frankie's arm.

She didn't try to defend herself. She looked up at him with those grey, black-fringed eyes. She didn't even cringe. She knew she was innocent; she knew she hadn't caused the monster or the storm.

She said, "Don't be afraid, Mr. Henson. We're gonna be all right, if we just stay quiet and keep our heads."

That must have made him feel foolish, a girl, not even twelve yet, being braver than he was. He dropped her arm and sat on the stairs, a few steps below her.

"We ain't gonna be all right. We all gonna die here in this house."

I had been thinking that same thought, but hearing this spineless man say those words made my old stubborn nature come back.

"We're not gonna die," I said.

Now that I had said those words aloud, I was determined to make my belief come true.

I turned to Frankie and cried, "We're not, are we, Frankie?"

Frankie lifted her chin and said, "No. Raymie's gonna come back and save us."

"Yeah," Tom snickered. "Miss Marcie's big, powerful, bean-brained brother's gonna save you from a hurricane. Listen, girlie, that pea-head couldn't protect a flea."

I was furious at his making fun of Raymie, but I decided I'd be smart to keep quiet. I'd said enough to get him riled up. Marcie and I sat on the landing, staring at the sheets of rain lashing the window.

The waiting was awful. The torrents of rain, the screaming, howling wind, the snapping, breaking, crashing, and wailing sounds never ceased. Every so often we would hear a window in the house breaking, the splintered glass shattering against the floors and walls.

I did a lot of wondering. I wondered when the water would cover the entire house. I wondered, maybe, if we could float away on boards, or even mattresses. I'd heard stories of people doing that in hurricanes.

I wondered if Mama and Papa had already been in the hurricane and were drowned. I wondered if Raymie had made it back to the bayou.

But I was determined to be brave, and I knew Frankie had made her mind up, too.

Every so often, Tom Henson would curse. I didn't like that. I said, "You oughta be ashamed of yourself, cussing in front of little girls." I didn't call myself *little* in front of most folks, but he was a grown man; he shouldn't talk like that in front of us.

Frankie said, "Yeah!"

He must have listened to us because, after a while, he stopped.

The storm was really getting to his nerves. He'd stand up, walk up the stairs, turn around in the hall, and come back down. As much as he seemed to dislike us I believe he was afraid to be by himself. I suppose he had been able to handle being alone before the storm got so bad, but now he seemed to need our company, even though we were children.

He insisted we light several more candles. I tried to convince him that wasn't a good idea.

"If we use them up now we won't have any for later," I said.

He ignored me and continued to light the candles, dripping wax on the cypress flooring of the landing to make them stand upright. I could see he was afraid to be in the dark, and although I knew this was foolish, I, too, felt more secure with the added light.

Suddenly, with no warning, he roared. He just stood up and bellowed. Frankie and I clutched one another in terror as he leaped about, threw his arms into the air, and began to rush down the steps. I don't know what he had in mind, but at that moment, I believe he was insane with fear.

I was even more stunned when Frankie quickly pushed me aside. She jumped up and leaped onto Tom's shoulders from the landing. I was stunned.

They both fell to the steps, but Frankie clutched the rail, even as she grasped Tom Henson's leg. She hung on to him as if his life depended upon it. I'll never know how they kept from tumbling to the bottom.

What was wrong with her? Had she lost her mind, too?

I stood to see what was happening. The light from all the candles brightened the stairs.

Then I saw the water moccasin.

His life *had* depended on her actions. The snake was on the third step of the stairs where the water had risen, several steps below where Tom and Frankie were clutching one another.

She had seen the snake and jumped to save Tom. He knelt there in openmouthed terror, clinging to Frankie.

The snake on the stairs below us opened its mouth. The pinkish-white inside looked like cotton, proving it was a water moccasin. It was about two or three feet long, with ten or twelve dark olive bands across his blackish body. His head was shaped like a triangle. It probably had swum up from the swampy woods way beyond the house; water moccasins aren't saltwater reptiles.

Tom and Frankie weren't out of danger yet. The moccasin could strike any moment. I had to act quickly. With all the strength I could muster I took aim and threw the candle I was holding at the snake. From the glow of the other candles on the landing I could see the candle made its mark.

The snake slid into the water and disappeared into the living room.

Tom and Frankie crawled back to the landing. They were both in shock. Tom's pants had been torn in the fall. One knee was skinned and bleeding. Frankie had hurt her ankle. I took one of the candles and went up the stairs to the bathroom where there was iodine and gauze.

Frankie said she didn't think her ankle was sprained. Together we bandaged Tom Henson's knee. He continued to look at us both with suspicion.

We were both in a daze. I couldn't believe we were helping this awful person. Worse, he didn't say even one word of thanks to either of us. It was as if we had done nothing to save him, as if we were supposed to bandage his wound.

That made us more afraid of him. A man who could suddenly go berserk was a man to fear. For the time being he was quiet, but his silence frightened us.

Puzzled, we watched as he sat on his haunches, silently rocking back and forth. Often he'd lift a candle high to stare at the steps below. Once in a while, he'd whimper. Maybe he was still in shock.

I looked at the face of the grandfather clock. Three-thirty. I never stayed up that late. I made up my mind. I wasn't going to sit here, watching that water rise and listening to Tom Henson's cowardly whimpers.

"Frankie," I said, "let's go to one of the bedrooms and lie down. I'm really tired, aren't you?"

Now that our unexplained fear of the upper rooms had appeared in the dreadful form of Tom Henson, the upstairs didn't seem as frightening.

We took several candles and the matches, and we headed for the upstairs bedrooms. Angry and almost begrudgingly, Tom moved his legs to let us pass.

"You know what I think, Miss Frankie Fedora?" he said. "I think you done caused that snake to come in this here house. Everybody know there ain't no moccasins in a bay."

Frankie had risked her life when she had tackled him. I had chased the snake away when I had thrown the candle. We had wrapped and bandaged his knee. This kind of thinking was strange to us. We were too stunned to reply.

Waiting Out the Storm

We stood in the hall for a moment, wondering which bedroom to enter. First we looked into a sort of dormitory. There was a row of eight beds in there. The Slades probably used this when they had a large number of guests visiting from Montgomery. Next to this was a smaller bedroom with twin beds.

Forlorn and discouraged, we flung ourselves across the twin beds. We had lost hope. There seemed to be no sign of the storm letting up; the rain and wind continued at a wild, unchecked pitch.

Downstairs, the water had risen to the fourth step. I knew now that Raymie would never be able to come for us, and although we no longer spoke of it, we both knew we may never see our friends and loved ones again.

Added to this was the terrible realization we were in this house with a crazed, ungrateful man. The problems seemed more than we could handle.

We tried to sleep, but a sudden burst of thunder, a flash of lightning, or abrupt changes in wind sounds from moans to wails made sleep impossible.

Frankie got off her bed and sat on the edge of mine. "What do you think he's doing?" she asked.

"I don't know," I said, "but I don't believe he'll go downstairs." I figured he wasn't about to take a chance of running into that snake again.

"Let's go see," she whispered.

I took her hand. We groped along the hall, tiptoeing to the top of the stairs. We leaned over the stair rail and peered at the landing below.

Tom wasn't there.

"Where do you think he could be?" I asked.

Just then a rough hand clasped the back of my neck. I knew the other hand had grabbed Frankie; I heard her frightened gasp.

In terror I twisted away from Tom Henson's tight grip. His wild and mindless laugh sent chills down my back and behind my knees.

"Scared you, didn't I?" he shrieked. Then, his voice low and threatening, he commanded, "Bring them candles in here!"

He pulled a small knife from his pants pocket and held it close to Frankie's back.

He insisted we go back into our room to pick up our candles. Once he had led us to the dormitory he insisted we light the candles and distribute them around the room. If a gust of wind escaped from the moldings of the windows and blew a candle out, he'd order us to relight it. He was becoming increasingly agitated.

Frankie and I chose two of the beds furthest away from Tom and dropped onto them. On another bed, Tom propped several pillows behind his head and fixed his eyes on the windows as if he were straining to see outside into the darkness and the rain.

I don't think he intended to sleep, but Frankie leaned across her bed and poked me. She pointed at him. His eyes were half-closed as if he had no intention of giving in to his tired body. His mouth was open, and he lightly snored.

"Should we go back to the other room?" Frankie whispered.

I thought a moment, then whispered back, "Nah, that might make him mad. He's scared of being alone. I guess there is nothing we can do but wait and see what's gonna happen to us. Frankie, are you praying?"

"'Course," she said.

"Me, too," I said.

We were quiet then. And who would have ever thought that three tired people, as frightened as we all were, would go to sleep in the middle of a raging storm?

I'm not sure how long we slept. I think it was about six when I woke up. The last time I'd noticed the grandfather clock it had read four o'clock. But the time of day wasn't the important point. It was the silence. The unnatural quiet awakened me. The only sound was the beautiful singing voices of many birds.

There was no wind. No rain. No crashing windows. No shuddering walls. The shutters of the house were closed, but through the slats I could see brightness shining through. A shimmering yellow.

I looked at the faces of Frankie and Tom Henson. They were both asleep. Quietly, I slipped out of the bed, went to the window, and opened the shutters.

I had never thought I would see a day like this again. The sky was a clear and startling blue. The water of the bay, now widened to make an island of the Slade's house, reflected a blue as true as the sky's. Across the face of it were a million diamond lights, reflecting the glimmering sun. I have never in my life seen anything as beautiful. Or as welcome.

I couldn't keep this miracle quiet. I banged the shutter doors loudly. Then I whirled and leaped about, landing in a heap on Frankie's bed.

"Frankie!" I shouted. "Wake up! Tom! It's over! It's over!" I began to cry with joy and relief. "Oh, thank God, the hurricane is over!"

Frankie sat up, dazed. She threw her arms around my neck. Across the room I saw Tom Henson sitting bolt upright, a stupid, alarmed expression on his face.

"Get up, Frankie!" I screamed, and when she did we clasped hands and danced about the room, not paying any attention to Tom Henson as we laughed and cried, "We're alive! We're alive! We didn't drown."

Tom Henson had rushed from the room. He was clattering down the stairs, screaming and shrieking, "I'm getting outta here! I'm going home!"

Frankie and I rushed to the top of the stairs to see what he was going to do. There he came, rushing back up the stairs at full speed.

"I can't get outta this here place!" he yelled. "There's still water all over the lawn. It's probably crawling with moccasins!"

For some reason that struck Frankie and me as the craziest thing we'd ever heard anyone say. We sat down at the top of the stairs and laughed until our faces were wet with tears.

Tom looked at us in dismay, but for some reason he didn't get angry. I suppose he was so glad the hurricane was over, so glad to see the beautiful daylight, that he just sat down on the landing below us and stared at us, confused.

Well, Frankie and I weren't confused any longer. We were going home, water moccasins or not.

Survivors

Tom Henson thought *we* were the crazy ones now. We knew we'd have to wait awhile before we could start the walk home. We knew no one could drive to pick us up until the water went down. Even the road was probably washed out in places, impossible for a car to get through. We also knew there may be no one alive to come, even if the roads were passable.

On this light, bright day we weren't as afraid of Tom Henson as we had been. Frankie probably worried about the things he'd say if we'd ever get back to a normal life in the bayou. I know I did. But I think we both decided we'd worry about those things later. Now we were so thankful to God that we were alive and well that we pushed these worries away.

So we straightened the beds. We scraped up the wax from the places where the candles had dripped. We ate a few more crackers and drank the rest of the apple juice. Then we picked up the crumbs we had dropped and walked across the slippery wet floors to return the cracker box to the kitchen. We found a mop and tried to wipe some of the water from the floors.

I couldn't figure out what had gotten into me. Mama was always telling me how important it was to be responsible. Even though the Slades didn't know we had taken shelter in their house, we were grateful to them.

"My mama would never believe me," I said to Frankie. "She'd give a million dollars to see me work like this at home."

"Mine, too," Frankie giggled. I liked hearing her giggle again.

Tom Henson continued to sit on the landing, sullen and angry.

"When we get outta here I'm gonna tell everybody in Bayou La Batre that you caused this storm, funny lips."

I was ready to tear into him for that cruel remark, but Frankie grabbed my fisted hand and said, "Don't pay him any mind, Marcie."

So I didn't. Frankie and I began to talk of going home.

"I don't think the water's too high now," I said, "and I don't imagine there are any snakes left. I think it was an accident that a moccasin got this far away from the woods and the creek. I hope."

Doubtful, she said, "Are you sure?"

I remembered then that she was a city girl. I don't suppose she had seen water moccasins in New Orleans.

"Well, no," I said. I couldn't be completely sure. "But we'll keep a sharp lookout."

We walked down the stairs past Tom Henson, who was still crouched on the landing.

"We're walking home," I said. "You can come if you wanna."

"Y'all are just crazy outta your mind," he said. He didn't move and we had to step over him to get down.

We opened the door and walked onto the porch. The water was slowly receding. The porch was wet, but now the water level was at the bottom steps off the screened porch outside.

As we walked through the ankle-deep water on the lawn we heard Tom yelling at us. "I know why y'all ain't afraid," he screamed. "It's cause you're in cahoots with beasts and reptiles like sea monsters and water moccasins."

Frankie sighed, and I shrugged.

"I guess we're gonna have to worry about him later," I said, "but Jeanné's family, and Hank's, and mine, we'll all stick by you."

I thought, *If they're alive,* but I didn't say it.

We sludged through mud, shells, dead fish and birds, driftwood, all kinds of debris. We saw no moccasins. Some of the small beach cottages were completely destroyed.

Now that the storm was over the day was humid. Our only relief was to dip into the water, but as soon as we stood, the stifling heat seemed to make breathing almost impossible.

As we passed the little peninsula we could see Raymie's old car down the shell lane. That poor Buick was lying on its side. From where we stood, it looked badly damaged.

My voice choked when I said, "It looks . . . dead."

We hoped Frankie's mother and father had survived in their brick house, but although Frankie tried to comfort me, I felt certain Mama and Papa hadn't made it, driving along the Gulf highway.

The more we talked, the more miserable we became.

"And, Frankie," I said. "I have to be prepared. I just know Raymie couldn't have made it home. I just know."

She put a comforting hand on my shoulder, but I couldn't be comforted.

"If Raymie's alive, I'll never be mean to him again," I vowed. "I won't tease him about his girl, and I'll let him call me shrimp as much as he wants."

Then a new thought came to me.

Jeanné. I wondered if she and her family had made it though the storm.

I said, "I'm so sorry I got mad with Jeanné for not believing me about the monster of the bayou. Frankie, you believe me, don't you?"

I was surprised when she paused a moment before she said, "Well, I sort of do, but Marcie, you really do have an amazing imagination."

That hurt. But it would have hurt even more if we hadn't had so many important people and things to worry about.

I took a deep breath and said, "If everybody's all right, I'm still gonna prove to you that the monster's real, Frankie."

She said, "You know something, I think you're probably right. If there could be a hurricane like that, and we could come out of it alive, like in a miracle, I don't know why there couldn't be a monster in the bayou."

I liked her for saying that.

Well, a lot of amazing things happened that day. Stupendous, really. First, as we came to the union of the bayou and the bay, we could actually see the road that paralleled the bayou. The tide hadn't gone down completely, but we were able to walk on the road, now a wet jumble of mud, sand, and crushed shells. At some places the road was washed out. We had to skirt it by climbing along the sides, but we no longer had to walk in the water.

At Rosie's Fresh Fish House we began to see a few people. They were walking out onto the road, dazed and unbelieving as they looked about at the effects of the storm. I was surprised to see Rosie's Fish House was standing, but it was badly damaged.

The house where Rosie lived was across the road from the fish house. I noticed the windows had all been boarded against the storm. She must have done that in a hurry.

She came out on her porch, and when she saw us she walked over to us.

"Marcie Delchamps," she exclaimed. "What are you doing up here? You look awful. Are you all right?"

"Yeah," I said, but I didn't want to talk about me. I wanted to know if she knew anything about my folks.

"Honey," she said, "I don't know anything about anyone. We been holed up in our house all night. But, near as I can see, the bayou crossed the road but didn't come into folks' houses, just the buildings on the bayou. Most of our homes are on a slight rise, you know."

We told her how we had gotten stranded and where we had spent the night. We asked if we could use her phone.

"Nah, sweetie, ain't any of the phones working. We ain't had power all night."

"Did Raymie come by to use your phone yesterday?" I asked, my heart in my mouth.

"No, honey," Rosie said, putting a comforting hand on my shoulder. "But don't worry. I'm sure your family's all right. I'd give you a lift to your house, but my car was covered up past the flooring. There's water in the gas."

Frankie and I said good-by and continued up the road. We were getting tired, but the worry about our families kept us going. I was in despair of ever seeing Raymie again. He may have drowned, and I knew it would be my fault for asking him to take us "around the coast" yesterday.

Home

As we came to Mr. Tolly's ice plant, we saw a boy, a teenager, coming around the bend in the road. He was walking with a fast and determined stride. All of a sudden I knew. The boy was Raymie.

He didn't see us. I have never been as happy to see anyone before or since. I screamed, and when Frankie saw why I screamed, she screamed, too.

"Raymie, Raymie!" I called, and I began to run. Frankie was close behind me.

Down the road, coming to us, Raymie ran, too. His arms were opened wide, the way Papa's would have been if he were there. I did the same thing. When we met we threw our arms around each other and held on tightly, saying one another's names over and over. We were both crying.

After a while Raymie stopped hugging me. He put his arms around Frankie and hugged her, too.

"I thought y'all were drowned," he said, "and I knew it was all my fault for taking you out on a day like that."

"No, no," Frankie and I both said. We told him we were to blame. After all, we'd begged him to take us.

I took a deep breath. I was afraid to ask him the most important question in the world.

"Have you—have you heard from Mama and Papa?"

"Oh, golly, Marcie. Of course, you couldn't know. They turned around and came back yesterday before they even crossed that big, ole long bridge at Pascagoula. They heard about the hurricane warnings. Got home right after I got back. But we couldn't get to you, either on foot or by car. I'm sure you saw how the coast roads were washed out. We didn't sleep all night, but when we saw the storm was over, I told Mama and Papa I'd go see. I had a terrible time with them all night. I practically had to hog-tie them to keep them from going, but I just knew they'd drown. Mama's been hysterical, of course."

He grinned and ducked his head in the way he did when he was embarrassed.

"I guess Papa and I were a little bit hysterical, too, come to think of it," he added.

I said, "Raymie, your car's ruined. We saw it out on the peninsula, turned over."

He shook his head, "Yeah, I figured."

Hesitantly, Frankie asked, "Have you heard anything from my folks?"

Raymie shook his head. "I'm sorry, Frankie, there aren't any phones working, but Mama and Papa are driving over to get them right now. He figured they should all be together when they found out about y'all. You see, we've been expecting the worst for you two. I don't think your folks were in any real danger, though. Other than the winds."

He was immediately sorry he'd said that, because Frankie murmured, "There are pine trees all around our house."

Raymie, not at all sure, said, "I'm sure they're all right, honey."

The three of us, all huddled together, walked home. There were many fallen trees, but it was as Miss Rosie had said—the bayou had risen, but not enough to go into the houses. Even so, many of the smaller shacks on the bayou itself were ruined or damaged.

Never had home looked so wonderful. Water still covered most of the yards, but we had waded through deeper water than this on the coast. We couldn't wait to get in the house.

The first thing we did was open the icebox. We ate cantaloupe and made toast. Raymie cooked us bacon and eggs.

I asked Frankie, "Isn't this the best breakfast you've ever had in your whole life?"

She laughed and said, "Nah, I like crackers and apple juice better."

Now that we had outlived a hurricane, we started having our giggling fits again.

When Mama and Papa and the Fedoras arrived, Frankie and I met them out front. We all hugged one another. There were more tears. More laughter. We were all so happy to know our families were alive.

We sat around our kitchen table while the grown-ups drank cup after cup of coffee. A person would have thought Frankie and I had been on some happy holiday. The fears and frustrations were pushed far back in our minds, but we told them about Tom Henson.

They shook their heads and said he was certainly a sick man. Neither Frankie nor I told of his particular insults to her. We didn't want to talk about that.

"Papa," I asked, "have you seen the bayou monster yesterday or early this morning?"

"Honey," Papa said, "there hasn't even been a boat out to cause a wake, believe me. Everybody's been staying home. All Raymie and I'll be doing today is sweeping out the water from the shop and drying out the merchandise. We were lucky our building's on such high pilings."

I have to say again—it was an amazing day. Our next visitor gave us an unbelievable gift.

While we were sitting there, each one telling about his or her adventures, there was a knock at the door.

Dr. Slade was there. I remembered him from when he'd visited our church. Mama asked him to join us for coffee. She brought him to the table and introduced everyone. Then he sat at the table with us.

"Are you the two little girls who stayed all night in our beach home?" he asked, nodding his head toward us.

I quickly looked at Frankie. What could he want? Was he upset with us?

He turned to our folks and said, "Mr. and Mrs. Delchamps, Mr. and Mrs. Fedora, y'all can be mighty proud of these two girls. You see, I arrived in Mobile last night during that terrible storm. I had planned to shut the place up for the season. Well, when I called the weather station they told me to stay put; I shouldn't try to make it to the bayou."

"Did we do something wrong?" I asked.

Everyone leaned forward with questioning eyes. *Had* we done something wrong?

"Wrong?" he exclaimed. "Not on your life! You see, I was determined to see if my house was ruined, so I spent the last couple of hours hiking over to it. But some crazy man was there. He kept raving on, something about water moccasins. He started telling me all about how y'all put everything up, and scraped the wax off the floors, and mopped up. Funny thing, he thought *you* were crazy, told me some crazy tale about a bayou monster. But I got the picture. I came to ask what I could do to thank you."

Our folks started saying all those nice things about being proud, the way parents do, so we began to feel proud ourselves.

Dr. Slade said he was determined to do something for us. What would we like? Frankie and I couldn't think of a thing to say for a long time.

But a wonderful thought came to me.

"Could I see you alone for a moment, Dr. Slade?" I asked.

Mama had a shocked, embarrassed expression in her face. She must have thought I was going to ask for a reward or something. She should have known me better than that.

"Of course," Dr. Slade said. He turned to the others and said, "Excuse us, please."

I didn't want anyone to hear, so I took him out to the swing on the front porch.

"Wanna sit down?" I said.

We both sat in the swing, lightly swaying it with our feet. The way his eyes smiled as he looked at me reminded me of Papa.

I didn't know how I was going to ask this, but I took a deep breath and said, "Someone tole me you're a doctor that can fix mistakes in people."

"Well, I guess you could call it that. I'm a surgeon," he said.

"Could you—uh—fix a harelip?" I asked. My heart was in my throat.

His eyes brightened. He smiled at me and put his arm around my shoulder. He said, "You're talking about your little friend, aren't you? I noticed her lip. Well, yes, we are learning there are things we can do about that."

I nodded my head furiously. My mouth was dry. I hoped he wouldn't get mad at me.

Softly, I said, "She really hates it, but she's real nice about it."

"Well, maybe we could do that for her. What about you? What do you want, Marcie?"

"Oh," I cried, "that *is* what I want. But I suppose it's asking a lot for just the few little things we did."

I was as selfish as any girl alive, but I knew that an operation for Frankie would be a wonderful gift for me, too.

So that's how this marvelous thing happened. When Dr. Slade went back in the kitchen he asked the Fedoras to go out to our porch swing with him. I sat back down at my place at the table.

I said, "Mama, could I have some café au lait?" That's half coffee and half milk. Mama was looking at me as if I had lost my mind. She got the café au lait.

Raymie said, "I sure hope you didn't ask for something expensive, Marcie."

I didn't say anything. I put two teaspoons of sugar in my café au lait and stirred like crazy. They'd find out soon enough.

After a while Dr. Slade and the Fedoras went their separate ways, but not until they had set up appointments for surgery in Montgomery.

There was a lot of hugging and kissing by every-one.

Raymie drove the Fedoras back home, and Mama started raking outside where the broken tree limbs and fallen leaves had made a terrible mess of our porch.

Papa went down to the shop, but he didn't stay for long. He came right back up to the house, calling for me.

"Marcie," he said, "I want you to come with me."

"What's the matter?" I asked.

Papa put his hand on my shoulder and said, "Nothing's the matter, Marcie. In fact, I have never been so proud of you. I just wanna show you something amazing. Just trust me."

We walked to the wharf. Water still covered the ramp, but we didn't get on the wharf. He led me over to the skiff that had somehow survived the storm.

"Get in, honey," he said.

We got in. Papa began to row across the bayou.

"Now look where I'm heading," he said.

There was my monster of the bayou, strung out on the other side of the bayou. I gasped.

"Why, he's dead, isn't he?" I asked.

But then I could see. This was no monster.

Papa slipped the boat up to the shell clear-ing where, on other days, fishermen tarred and mended their nets. Spread across the shore was my bayou monster, ten rubber car tires strung together with rope. At one end, a length of the rope was shaggy and unraveled. Like a tail. On the other end was a red flag. A red tongue, or a flame of dragon fire. I felt foolish. I felt stupid.

"Oh, Papa," I cried. "I'm so ashamed. I really did think it was a sea monster. I did. I wasn't making it up . . ."

"I know," he said, "and I can certainly see why you thought that. I'm sure if I had ever seen it, I would've been fooled, too."

"Well, what is it?" I asked. "Did someone try to trick us?"

"No," he said. "You know how those big barges come in to dredge the bayou to make it wider and deeper? Well, they string these tires on the sides to keep the barge from scraping wharves or other boats. Evidently a part of one of these strings broke loose."

"Oh, Papa . . ." I sighed. "I caused so much trouble."

"Hey," Papa said softly, "a lot of other folks were fooled, too. You see, the tires would only rise up when a boat with a strong engine made a wake."

"Tom Henson," I said. "We have to be sure Tom Henson sees this."

"Yeah," Papa said. "Well, we've solved the monster, so we might as well go back home."

In a way I was disappointed the monster hadn't been real. Papa must have read my thoughts, because as he rowed me back, he said, "You know, honey, I can easily see why you thought that rigamarole was a monster, and, in a way, he *was* real. Your hale and hearty imagination just gave him the breath of life. Well, he's dead now. But someday you'll remember the good times you had with him. It's sort of a gift your Creator has given you."

That was a strange thing to say.

"A *gift*? How, Papa?"

"How the good times stay in our memories and become stronger in our minds, and the bad almost fades away."

Papa was right. Everything worked out fine, and I have a lot of fun remembering things now.

I was happy to know Jeanné, and Hank, and their families survived the storm.

Frankie had her operation. Her lip wasn't completely perfect, but she looked much better. Dr. Slade did a great job. He and Frankie were written up in the *American Medical Journal*. I have a great picture of them in my scrapbook.

Tom Henson admitted he was wrong about Frankie. I got to be there and see his expression when he saw my rubber tire monster.

Come to think of it, some of my very best memories are of the bayou monster and the hurricane.

About the Author

Betty Hager never saw a monster in the bayou on which she lived, but the idea of sea monsters fascinated her as a child. She does remember being on the "edge" of a few hurricanes. And she did know a woman with a harelip and remembers feeling deep sympathy for her.

Betty was eight years old when she became hooked on writing. Although she majored in writing at the University of Alabama, she didn't pursue her writing in earnest until years later. When the youngest of her three sons graduated from high school, she wrote *Old Jake and the Pirate's Treasure* and also began to write children's musicals.

Marcie and the Monster of the Bayou is the fourth book in the Tales from the Bayou series. Betty hopes you will read all four books about Marcie and her older brother, Raymie.

Betty loves to hear from her readers. You may write her at this address:

Betty Hager
Author Relations
Zondervan Publishing House
Grand Rapids, MI 49530

Look for more of Marcie's adventures!

Old Jake and the Pirate's Treasure
Book 1 $4.99 0-310-38401-X

Is Old Jake really hiding a pirate's treasure map?
Marcie, Raymie, and Hank decide to find out —
by sneaking inside Old Jake's house! They're on
to a mystery and more ...

Miss Tilly and the Haunted Mansion
Book 2 $4.99 0-310-38411-7

Marcie imagines all sorts of things, like maybe
Miss Tilly really is a witch. When her mother
makes her visit Miss Tilly, some terrifying
adventures and a new friend await her ...

Marcie and the Shrimp Boat Adventure
Book 3 $4.99 0-310-38421-4

Marcie's brother gets to do so much — like go
sailing on the shrimp boat. So when Marcie finally
gets on board, she's overjoyed. But soon she finds
she needs a miracle to get out alive ...

Marcie and the Monster of the Bayou
Book 4 $4.99 0-310-38431-1

Marcie is sure she saw a monster, but the only
person who doesn't laugh is also telling awful
stories about Marcie's new friend. Soon Marcie
must face a bigger enemy — a hurricane.